Shadows of the Heartstone

A Tale of Courage and Unity in the Face of Darkness

Morgan Logstone

First Edition: June 2024

Table of Contents

Chapter 1
The Village of Shadows

The village lay nestled in a valley, shrouded in a perpetual twilight that whispered of ancient curses and looming shadows. The villagers lived in constant fear, their lives governed by superstitions and the ever-present threat of the shadow realm. Conversations were hushed, and eyes darted nervously to the dark forest that bordered their home. Each day, the villagers would gather in the market square, selling their goods quickly before retreating to the safety of their homes, their minds haunted by the unknown forces at play.

"Did you hear about the fire at the well?" whispered Thomas, a blacksmith, to his friend Edgar, a farmer. They stood by the edge of the market, their voices low and their faces etched with worry.

"Aye, Elara was there," Edgar replied, glancing around as if expecting to see something emerge from the shadows. "They say she's cursed, that she brought the shadows upon us."

Thomas shuddered. "I've heard the same. She lives alone out there, near the Forbidden Forest. It's unnatural, what she can do."

The whispers spread like wildfire through the village. The well, now a charred ruin, stood as a grim reminder of the incident. Villagers hurried past it, casting wary glances at the blackened stone. Children were pulled closer by their parents, who whispered warnings about the cursed girl on the outskirts.

At the center of the market square, the village elder, Maester Joren, addressed a small gathering. His voice, though aged, carried a weight of authority. "We must remain vigilant," he warned. "The shadow realm is always watching, always waiting. We cannot afford to let fear divide us."

"But what about Elara?" a woman called out from the crowd. "She's dangerous! We can't just ignore what happened at the well."

Joren sighed heavily. "Elara is a troubled soul, but we must not let fear drive us to rash actions. We must seek to understand before we judge."

The crowd murmured in reluctant agreement, but the unease remained palpable. As the market began to disperse, the villagers returned to their homes, their conversations filled with speculation and fear. The incident at the well had shaken them deeply, and the shadow of suspicion hung over Elara like a dark cloud.

In the dim light of the setting sun, Thomas and Edgar walked back to their homes, their faces still drawn with worry. "We need to do something about her," Thomas said, his voice low.

"We can't just drive her away," Edgar replied, though his tone was uncertain. "She's still one of us, isn't she?"

Thomas shook his head. "Not anymore. She's dangerous. We have to protect our families."

As they parted ways, the village settled into an uneasy silence. Night fell, and the forest seemed to creep closer, its shadows reaching out like dark tendrils. In their homes, the villagers locked their doors and whispered prayers, hoping to keep the darkness at bay for one more night.

The next morning, as the first light of dawn struggled to pierce the thick fog, the villagers awoke to the same pervasive sense of dread. Mothers held their children a little tighter, and men exchanged uneasy glances as they prepared for another day. The fear of the unknown, of the shadow realm and its influence, weighed heavily on their minds.

Thomas, preparing his forge for the day's work, glanced toward the edge of the village where Elara lived. "We can't keep living like this," he muttered to himself. "Something has to change."

Meanwhile, Edgar stood in his field, turning over the soil with a heavy heart. The crops had been poor this season, and he couldn't shake the feeling that the village's troubles were only beginning. "It's the curse," he whispered, his eyes narrowing as he looked toward the forest. "It's all because of her."

On the outskirts of the village, Elara lived a solitary existence. Her small, weathered hut was hidden near the edge of the Forbidden Forest, a place where few dared to venture. The villagers' fear had long since turned to hostility, isolating her further. She spent her days foraging in the forest and tending to her modest garden, trying to avoid the gaze of those who would shun her.

Elara stood at the edge of the forest, her green eyes reflecting the flickering light of her small fire. She sighed, pulling her cloak tighter against the chill. Her powers, dark and uncontrollable, had marked her as an outcast. She reached out a hand, and a small flame danced on her palm, casting eerie shadows on the trees around her.

"I didn't mean to," she whispered to herself, eyes filling with tears. "I just wanted to help."

Her only solace came from Lila, her childhood friend, who braved the villagers' scorn to bring her food and supplies. Lila approached quietly, her red hair glowing in the firelight. She carried a basket of freshly baked bread and cheese, a rare treat for Elara.

"Elara, you have to be more careful," Lila said gently, placing the basket on the ground. "The villagers are terrified. They don't understand."

Elara extinguished the flame and looked at Lila with a mixture of gratitude and sorrow. "I know, Lila. But I can't control it. It's like a curse."

Lila knelt beside her friend, her green eyes filled with compassion. "We'll find a way to help you, Elara. You just have to stay strong."

Elara nodded, though the weight of her isolation pressed heavily on her heart. She longed for acceptance, for a place where she could belong without fear. But each day seemed to push her further from that dream.

The forest around them rustled with unseen life, and Elara felt a strange kinship with its hidden creatures. Like her, they lived on the edges, unseen and misunderstood. She drew strength from the wild, untamed beauty of the woods, finding moments of peace amidst the chaos of her existence.

"Do you remember when we used to play in the fields?" Lila asked, breaking the silence. "Before all of this?"

Elara smiled faintly, the memory bittersweet. "I do. It feels like a lifetime ago."

Lila reached out and took Elara's hand. "We'll get through this, Elara. You're not alone."

As the night deepened, the two friends sat by the fire, their bond a small beacon of light in the encroaching darkness. Elara knew that Lila's loyalty was a rare gift, and she clung to it like a lifeline. Despite the fear and suspicion of the villagers, she found hope in their friendship, a fragile thread that kept her from succumbing to despair.

"I wish things were different," Elara murmured, staring into the flames. "I wish I could control this power."

Lila squeezed her hand gently. "We'll find a way. There's got to be someone who can help you, someone who understands."

Elara nodded, though doubt gnawed at her. "I hope so, Lila. I really hope so."

The forest around them seemed to whisper in agreement, the rustling leaves and swaying branches creating a symphony of hope and promise. For a moment, Elara allowed herself to believe that there might be a way out of the darkness, a way to reclaim her place in the village and live without fear.

As the fire crackled and the night grew colder, Elara and Lila sat in silence, drawing strength from each other's presence. The journey ahead was uncertain, but they faced it together, determined to find a way to break the curse and restore the light to their lives.

One bitter winter night, Elara ventured into the village to draw water from the well. The cold seeped into her bones, and her breath formed clouds in the frigid air. She wrapped her cloak tightly around herself, but her hands shook as she pulled the bucket from the well. The well, now repaired, stood as a reminder of the fire that had nearly destroyed it.

In her frustration and fear, her uncontrolled powers flared. Dark flames erupted around the well, the water boiling and hissing. The villagers, already on edge, rushed to the scene, their faces masks of terror and anger.

"She's done it again!" shouted Thomas, pointing an accusing finger at Elara. "She's bringing the curse upon us!"

Elara's heart pounded as she backed away, the flames still dancing around her. "No, I didn't mean to! Please, believe me!" she pleaded, her voice trembling with desperation.

"Get her away from here!" Edgar bellowed, advancing on Elara with a menacing look. "We can't have her causing more trouble."

"I don't want to hurt anyone!" Elara cried, her eyes wide with fear and sorrow.

The crowd closed in, their anger and fear fueling their actions. "She's a menace!" a woman shouted. "Look at what she's done!"

Lila burst through the crowd, her face flushed with urgency. "Stop! She's not doing this on purpose!" she cried, trying to shield Elara with her own body.

"Move aside, Lila," Thomas growled. "She needs to be stopped before she burns down the whole village."

Lila stood her ground, her eyes blazing with determination. "Elara is my friend. I won't let you harm her."

The tension reached a boiling point, and for a moment, it seemed as if violence would erupt. But then Maester Joren arrived, his presence calming the crowd. "Enough," he commanded, his voice firm. "This is not the way."

The villagers hesitated, their anger cooling under the elder's stern gaze. Elara, trembling and tearful, looked up at Joren with desperate eyes. "I didn't mean to," she whispered. "I can't control it."

Joren sighed, his expression softening. "I know, child. We must find a way to help you."

"Help her? She's a danger to us all!" Thomas protested. "We can't just let her roam free."

"Thomas, we cannot allow fear to cloud our judgment," Joren replied. "We must seek to understand before we judge."

"But she set the well on fire!" another villager shouted. "What's next? The whole village?"

"I'll leave," Elara said suddenly, her voice breaking. "I'll go far away, where I can't hurt anyone."

Lila grabbed her hand. "No, Elara. We can find another way."

Maester Joren raised a hand. "Elara, running away won't solve anything. We need to face this together. The village needs to come together, not be torn apart by fear."

The crowd murmured, uncertainty and fear mingling with a reluctant acceptance. "What can we do?" Edgar asked, his voice softer now.

Joren looked at Elara with a kind but serious expression. "We need to understand her powers and find a way to control them. We cannot act out of ignorance and fear."

"I'll help her," Lila said firmly. "I'll do whatever it takes."

"Thank you, Lila," Elara whispered, tears streaming down her face. "I don't know what I would do without you."

The villagers slowly began to disperse, their anger tempered by the elder's words and Lila's fierce loyalty. Elara and Lila made their way back to the edge of the village, the weight of the villagers' judgment heavy on their shoulders.

"Thank you, Lila," Elara said quietly, once they were out of earshot. "I don't know what I would do without you."

Lila squeezed her hand. "You don't have to thank me, Elara. We're friends. We'll figure this out together."

As they walked back to Elara's hut, the night seemed darker than usual, the shadows deeper and more oppressive. Elara couldn't shake the feeling that something was watching her from the forest, its unseen eyes following her every move. The incident at the well had only heightened her sense of foreboding, and she wondered how much longer she could endure the villagers' fear and suspicion.

Back at her hut, Elara sat by the fire, staring into the flames. "I have to find a way to control this," she said to herself, determination hardening her voice. "I can't keep living like this."

The fire at the well had revealed Elara's powers to the entire village. Her green eyes, glowing with the power of darkness and fire, became a symbol of their fear. She fled back to her hut, the weight of their judgment heavy on her heart. Inside her small home, she collapsed onto her bed, tears streaming down her face.

"Why can't I control it?" she sobbed, her voice barely a whisper. The flickering light of the fire cast long shadows on the walls, echoing her despair.

As she lay there, exhausted and defeated, she felt a flicker of resolve. She couldn't continue living like this, in fear and isolation. She had to find a way to control her powers, to break the curse that bound her. Little did she know, her journey was about to intertwine with that of a noble knight from the shadow realm, setting in motion events that would change both their worlds forever.

In the quiet of her hut, Elara made a silent vow. She would seek out the knowledge and the strength to master her powers. She would prove to the villagers that she was not their enemy, but a force for good. The path ahead was uncertain, and the shadows of the forest seemed to whisper of trials yet to come. But for the first time in a long while, Elara felt a spark of hope.

Outside, the wind howled through the trees, and the shadows danced with the promise of a destiny that awaited her. The journey to break the curse and find her placc in the world had just begun.

As dawn approached, Elara rose from her bed and began to prepare for the day. She packed a small bag with essentials, her movements deliberate and steady. She would seek out Elder Brynn, the wise old man who lived deep in the Forbidden Forest. He was said to have knowledge of ancient magic and curses, and perhaps he could help her understand her powers.

With a final glance around her hut, Elara stepped outside, the early morning light casting a soft glow on the frost-covered ground. She took a deep breath, steeling herself for the journey ahead. As she walked towards the forest, her heart was a mixture of fear and determination. The path was uncertain, but she knew she could not turn back.

"Lila," she whispered, more to herself than to the empty air. "I hope you understand why I have to do this."

Elara paused at the edge of the forest, looking back at the village she had known all her life. The memories, both good and bad, filled her with a sense of finality. She was leaving behind the only home she had ever known, stepping into the unknown in search of answers.

"I'll be back," she vowed quietly. "I won't let this curse define me."

With that, Elara plunged into the forest, the trees closing around her like a shroud. The journey ahead was fraught with danger, but she was resolved to face it head-on. She had to find a way to break the curse, not just for herself, but for the village and for Lila. The shadows whispered of trials and tribulations, but also of hope and redemption. And so, with determination in her heart, Elara began her quest.

Chapter 2
The Arrival of the Knight

In the shadow realm, darkness reigned supreme, its eerie silence broken only by the whispers of unseen entities. Sir Gareth knelt before the Shadow King, his heart heavy with the weight of the mission he was about to undertake. The Shadow King's throne room was a vast, cavernous space, illuminated by the dim glow of enchanted torches. The air was thick with the scent of ancient magic and the faint rustle of unseen creatures.

"Gareth," the Shadow King's voice echoed through the chamber, cold and commanding. "You have been chosen for a task of great importance. There is a threat in the human realm that must be eliminated."

Gareth looked up, his piercing blue eyes meeting the Shadow King's gaze. "What is this threat, my lord?"

The Shadow King leaned forward, his dark eyes gleaming with an intensity that made Gareth's skin crawl. "A young woman named Elara possesses powers that could disrupt the balance between our realms. She must be dealt with."

Gareth's heart pounded in his chest. "What kind of powers?"

"Dark powers," the Shadow King replied, his voice dripping with disdain. "Powers that she cannot control, powers that pose a danger to both her world and ours."

Gareth swallowed hard, his mind racing. "And what am I to do, my lord?"

"You are to cross into the human realm, find this girl, and eliminate the threat she poses," the Shadow King said, his tone final. "Do not let your emotions cloud your judgment. This is a matter of duty and necessity."

Gareth nodded, his resolve hardening. "I understand, my lord. I will not fail you."

The Shadow King waved his hand dismissively. "Go now, Gareth. The portal awaits."

As Gareth rose to his feet and turned to leave, he couldn't shake the feeling of unease that settled over him. He had faced many dangers in his service to the Shadow King, but this mission felt different. The weight of the task ahead pressed heavily on his shoulders as he made his way to the portal chamber.

The portal chamber was a dark, stone-walled room filled with the hum of ancient magic. A shimmering, swirling vortex of energy dominated the center of the chamber, casting an ethereal glow on the walls. Gareth took a deep breath, steeling himself for the journey ahead. He stepped into the portal, feeling the familiar pull of magic as he was transported to the human realm.

He emerged on the outskirts of the village, the air cold and biting against his skin. The village lay before him, shrouded in mist and shadow. He could hear the distant murmur of voices and the occasional cry of a child. Gareth's heart ached at the thought of what he might have to do, but he pushed the feeling aside. Duty came first.

"I must find her," he whispered to himself, his breath forming clouds in the frigid air. "I must complete my mission."

As he made his way through the village, Gareth couldn't help but notice the fear etched on the faces of the villagers. They moved quickly, avoiding his gaze and whispering to one another in hushed tones. He knew that finding Elara would not be easy, but he was determined to succeed.

Gareth crossed the mystical portal into the human realm, stepping into the fog-shrouded village. His armor gleamed darkly in the twilight, and his heart was heavy with the burden of his duty. The portal's magic left a lingering tingling sensation on his skin, a reminder of the otherworldly power that had brought him here.

He walked through the narrow, cobblestone streets, his senses alert for any sign of the girl he had been sent to find. The village was eerily quiet, the usual sounds of daily life muted by the pervasive sense of fear. Gareth could feel the weight of the villagers' eyes on him, their suspicion and anxiety palpable.

He stopped by a small shop, its windows darkened and the door slightly ajar. A woman peered out from behind the counter, her eyes wide with apprehension. Gareth approached her, his voice calm and authoritative.

"Good evening, madam," he said, inclining his head slightly. "I am looking for someone. A young woman named Elara. Do you know where I might find her?"

The woman's eyes darted nervously around the shop. "Elara? Why would you be looking for her?"

Gareth sensed her fear and softened his tone. "I mean her no harm. I just need to speak with her."

The woman hesitated, then nodded toward the edge of the village. "She lives on the outskirts, near the Forbidden Forest. But be careful, sir. She's... different."

"Thank you," Gareth replied, offering her a reassuring smile. "I appreciate your help."

As he continued his search, he couldn't help but wonder what kind of power this girl possessed that had drawn the attention of the Shadow King. The villagers' fear was evident, but Gareth couldn't shake the feeling that there was more to Elara's story than he had been told.

He made his way to the edge of the village, the mist thickening as he approached the forest. The trees loomed tall and foreboding, their branches twisted and gnarled like the fingers of some ancient, malevolent being. Gareth paused, listening to the sounds of the forest – the rustle of leaves, the distant hoot of an owl, and the faint, rhythmic sound of breathing.

He followed the sound, his footsteps silent on the forest floor. The mist parted to reveal a small, weathered hut, its windows glowing with the warm light of a fire. Gareth approached cautiously, his hand resting on the hilt of his sword. He could see a figure moving inside, her silhouette dancing in the flickering light.

"Elara?" he called out softly, hoping not to startle her. "I need to speak with you."

The door creaked open, and Elara stepped out, her green eyes wide with surprise and fear. "Who are you?" she demanded, her voice trembling.

"My name is Gareth," he said, his tone gentle but firm. "I have been sent to find you. We need to talk."

Elara's eyes narrowed, suspicion and curiosity warring within her. "Who sent you? Why are you here?"

Gareth took a deep breath, choosing his words carefully. "I come from the shadow realm. I was sent by the Shadow King to... deal with the threat you pose. But I don't believe you are a threat. I want to understand your powers and help you if I can."

Elara stared at him, her expression a mix of fear and hope. "Why would you want to help me? No one else does."

"Because I believe there is more to you than what I have been told," Gareth replied, his eyes meeting hers. "Please, let me help you."

The silence stretched between them, the weight of their shared uncertainty hanging in the air. Finally, Elara nodded, a single tear sliding down her cheek. "Alright, Gareth. But know this: my powers are dangerous, and I don't fully understand them myself. If you still want to help, then come inside. We have much to discuss."

As they stepped into the warmth of the hut, Gareth felt a strange sense of hope. Perhaps, together, they could find a way to control Elara's powers and protect both their worlds from the darkness that threatened to consume them.

Gareth found Elara by the smoldering well, her face pale and frightened. Seeing her vulnerability, he hesitated, struck by the innocence in her eyes. She was not the monster he had expected. As he approached, Elara stepped back, her eyes wide with fear and mistrust.

"Who are you?" she demanded, her voice shaking. "Why are you here?"

"My name is Gareth," he replied, keeping his tone calm and non-threatening. "I was sent to find you."

"Sent? By whom?" Elara's eyes narrowed, suspicion evident.

"The Shadow King," Gareth admitted, watching her reaction closely. "But not for the reasons you might think."

Elara took another step back, her hands trembling. "He sent you to kill me, didn't he? Everyone wants me dead."

Gareth shook his head, feeling a pang of guilt. "Yes, that was my mission. But I don't believe you are the threat they say you are. I want to help you."

"Help me?" Elara laughed bitterly. "Why would you help someone like me? No one else ever has."

"Because I've seen enough to know that things aren't always as they seem," Gareth said earnestly. "Please, let me understand what's happening. I need to know more about your powers."

Elara's eyes softened slightly, but she remained wary. "You really think you can help me? What if I hurt you too?"

Gareth stepped closer, his gaze steady. "I'm willing to take that risk. You don't have to face this alone."

The sincerity in his voice seemed to reach her. Elara glanced around, then back at Gareth. "Alright," she said quietly. "But we can't stay here. The villagers…"

Gareth nodded, understanding her fear. "We'll go somewhere safe. Lead the way."

They moved cautiously through the village, sticking to the shadows. Elara led Gareth to a secluded part of the forest, where the trees formed a natural barrier against prying eyes. They reached a small clearing, hidden from view, and sat down on a fallen log.

"Now, tell me everything," Gareth urged gently. "When did you first notice your powers?"

Elara took a deep breath, gathering her thoughts. "It started when I was little. Strange things would happen around me. Fires would start, things would move on their own. My parents tried to hide it, but after they died, the villagers began to notice. They were afraid, and I didn't know how to control it."

"And the fire at the well?" Gareth asked, his expression sympathetic.

"That was an accident," Elara said, her voice trembling. "I was just trying to get water, but I was so angry and scared. The flames just… erupted. I didn't mean for it to happen."

Gareth nodded, absorbing her words. "It sounds like your powers are linked to your emotions. That's not uncommon with magic. Have you ever tried to learn control?"

Elara shook her head. "No one would teach me. I've been alone for so long, just trying to survive. I'm afraid of hurting people."

Gareth reached out, placing a hand on her arm. "You're not alone anymore. I'll help you, Elara. We'll figure this out together."

Elara looked at him, hope flickering in her eyes. "Why are you doing this, Gareth? You don't even know me."

"I know enough," Gareth replied, his voice firm. "I've seen the fear and hatred in the eyes of those who misunderstand. I won't let that happen to you."

They sat in silence for a moment, the weight of Gareth's words settling over them. Elara felt a warmth she hadn't known in years—a sense of safety, however fragile it might be. She glanced at Gareth, his resolve clear.

"Thank you," she whispered. "For believing in me."

Gareth smiled, a small but genuine gesture. "We'll start by finding someone who can teach you control. There must be someone with knowledge of magic in this world. Together, we'll find a way."

As the sun began to set, casting long shadows over the forest, Elara felt a glimmer of hope. For the first time, she wasn't facing her fears alone.

Beat 4: Decision to Protect

Instead of killing her, Gareth decided to protect Elara and learn more about the curse that bound her. He saw potential in her, a chance to change both their worlds. His decision marked the beginning of their reluctant partnership.

"We need to move," Gareth said, glancing around the clearing. "The villagers will come looking for you soon. Do you know a place where we can hide?"

Elara nodded, her face resolute. "There's a cave deeper in the forest. It's hidden, and no one goes there."

"Lead the way," Gareth said, standing up and offering her a hand.

As they made their way through the dense forest, Elara glanced at Gareth, curiosity in her eyes. "Why did you change your mind? You were sent to kill me."

Gareth sighed, running a hand through his dark hair. "Because I believe you're more than what they say. I've seen enough darkness in my life to know when someone is truly evil. You're not."

Elara looked away, her expression troubled. "But what if I lose control again? What if I hurt you?"

"Then I'll help you regain control," Gareth replied firmly. "We'll figure this out together. I promise."

They walked in silence for a while, the sounds of the forest enveloping them. Finally, they reached the cave, its entrance hidden behind a thick curtain of ivy. Elara pushed the ivy aside and led Gareth inside. The cave was cool and dark, but spacious enough for them to rest.

"This will do," Gareth said, inspecting the cave. "We'll need supplies. I'll go back to the village tonight and gather what we need."

Elara's eyes widened in fear. "But it's dangerous. What if they catch you?"

"I'll be careful," Gareth assured her. "I've handled worse. Just stay here and rest. I'll be back before dawn."

Elara nodded reluctantly, watching as Gareth turned to leave. "Be safe," she whispered.

Gareth paused at the entrance, looking back at her. "I will. And Elara, remember, you're not alone anymore. We'll get through this."

With that, he disappeared into the night, leaving Elara alone in the cave. She sat down, pulling her cloak tightly around her, trying to calm the turmoil inside her. Gareth's words echoed in her mind, a small beacon of hope in the darkness.

Hours passed, and Elara dozed fitfully, waking at every sound. She was starting to worry when she heard footsteps outside the cave. Her heart raced, but relief flooded through her when she saw Gareth's silhouette.

He entered the cave, carrying a bundle of supplies. "I managed to get some food, blankets, and a few other things we might need," he said, setting the bundle down.

"Thank you," Elara said, her voice soft. "I was starting to think something happened to you."

"I'm fine," Gareth replied with a reassuring smile. "Now, let's make a plan. We need to find someone who can help you control your powers. Do you know anyone who might have that kind of knowledge?"

Elara thought for a moment. "There's an old hermit, Elder Brynn. He lives in the deepest part of the forest. The villagers say he's a wise man with knowledge of ancient magic."

"Then we'll go to him," Gareth decided. "At first light, we'll set out to find Elder Brynn. He might be the key to understanding your powers and breaking this curse."

Elara nodded, feeling a renewed sense of determination. "I hope he can help us."

Gareth looked at her, his expression serious but kind. "He will. And even if he can't, we'll find another way. I won't let anything happen to you, Elara."

As they settled down for the night, Gareth kept a watchful eye on the cave entrance, his thoughts racing. He had made a promise to protect Elara, and he intended to keep it. The journey ahead would be fraught with danger, but he was ready to face it. For the first time in his life, he felt a sense of purpose that went beyond duty—a purpose tied to the girl who had become his unexpected ally.

Chapter 3
The Prophecy Unveiled

Elara and Gareth journeyed deeper into the forest, the dense canopy above them blocking out much of the daylight. The path was treacherous, the ground uneven and littered with roots and rocks. Despite the challenges, they pressed on, determined to find Elder Brynn, the hermit who might hold the key to Elara's powers.

"Do you really think he'll help us?" Elara asked, her voice tinged with uncertainty.

Gareth nodded confidently. "Elder Brynn is known for his wisdom. If anyone can help, it's him."

Elara sighed, her breath visible in the chilly air. "I hope you're right. I'm tired of living in fear."

They continued in silence for a while, the only sounds being the rustling of leaves and the occasional bird call. The forest felt alive around them, almost as if it were watching their progress.

"Elara," Gareth said suddenly, breaking the silence. "Tell me more about your powers. How do they feel when they manifest?"

Elara hesitated, then spoke softly. "It's like a surge of energy, uncontrollable and wild. It's linked to my emotions. The stronger the emotion, the more intense the power."

Gareth looked thoughtful. "It makes sense. Emotional magic can be the most volatile. Controlling your feelings might be the key to controlling your powers."

"But how?" Elara asked, frustration creeping into her voice. "I've tried. It's like trying to hold back a storm with my bare hands."

Gareth reached out, gently touching her arm. "We'll find a way. Together."

Elara gave him a small, grateful smile. "Thank you, Gareth. I don't know what I'd do without you."

As they walked, the forest grew darker and more foreboding. The trees seemed to close in around them, their branches twisted and gnarled. Just when Elara thought they might be lost, they stumbled upon a small clearing. In the center stood a modest hut, smoke curling from its chimney.

"This must be it," Gareth said, relief evident in his voice.

They approached the hut cautiously. Gareth knocked on the door, the sound echoing in the quiet forest. Moments later, the door creaked open, revealing an old man with a long white beard and piercing blue eyes.

"Elder Brynn?" Gareth asked respectfully.

The old man nodded, his eyes studying them intently. "Who are you, and what brings you to my home?"

"My name is Gareth, and this is Elara," he replied. "We seek your wisdom. Elara has powers she cannot control, and we believe you might be able to help."

Elder Brynn's gaze shifted to Elara, his expression unreadable. "Powers, you say? Come inside. We have much to discuss."

Inside the hut, the air was warm and fragrant with the scent of herbs. The walls were lined with shelves filled with books, scrolls, and various magical artifacts. Brynn gestured for them to sit at a small wooden table.

"Elara," he began, his voice gentle but firm. "Tell me about your powers."

Elara took a deep breath, then explained everything—the fires, the fear, the inability to control her emotions. Brynn listened intently, nodding occasionally.

"Your powers are indeed formidable," he said thoughtfully. "And dangerous if left unchecked. But I sense something else—an ancient magic intertwined with your own."

"What do you mean?" Elara asked, her eyes wide with curiosity.

"There is a prophecy," Brynn explained. "One that speaks of a girl with dark powers and a knight destined to change the fate of their worlds. I believe you are that girl, Elara."

Elara felt a chill run down her spine. "A prophecy? What does it say?"

Brynn stood and retrieved an old, weathered scroll from a shelf. He unrolled it carefully, revealing intricate symbols and ancient text. "It speaks of a curse and a bond that must be formed to break it. You and Gareth are bound by fate. Together, you have the power to restore balance."

Gareth exchanged a look with Elara, his expression a mix of determination and concern. "How do we fulfill this prophecy?"

Brynn smiled, a twinkle in his eye. "That, my young friends, is a journey only you can take. But I will guide you as best I can."

Elder Brynn's hut was filled with the scent of burning herbs, casting a soothing atmosphere over the room. Elara and Gareth sat across from the old man, absorbing the weight of his words. The revelation of the prophecy had shifted their understanding of their mission entirely.

"Elara, your powers are not just a curse. They are a key," Brynn said, his voice steady. "A key to a greater destiny."

Elara looked at Brynn, her eyes wide with hope and fear. "But how can I control something so volatile? Every time I try, it ends in disaster."

Brynn nodded thoughtfully. "Control comes from understanding. We must delve into the origins of your powers. Do you know anything about your lineage?"

Elara shook her head. "My parents never spoke of it. They died when I was young."

The elder sighed. "Often, power of this magnitude is inherited. There may be answers in your family's past."

Gareth leaned forward, his expression serious. "We need to find those answers. Is there a place we can start?"

Brynn stroked his beard, contemplating. "There are ancient ruins in the deepest part of this forest. They hold secrets and might contain the knowledge you seek. But be warned, the journey is perilous."

Elara's determination hardened. "I don't care about the danger. I need to understand who I am and why this is happening."

Gareth nodded in agreement. "We'll face it together. Tell us more about these ruins."

Brynn's eyes darkened slightly. "The ruins are remnants of an ancient civilization that dabbled in powerful magic. They are protected by enchantments and creatures born of the shadows. But within, you may find texts or artifacts that reveal your heritage."

Elara glanced at Gareth, finding reassurance in his steady presence. "We have to go. This could be the key to everything."

Brynn rose and walked to a shelf, retrieving a small, intricately carved box. "Take this," he said, handing it to Gareth. "It's an amulet of protection. It will shield you from some of the dangers you will face."

Gareth accepted the amulet, slipping it over his head. "Thank you, Elder Brynn. We'll make sure it's put to good use."

Brynn smiled warmly. "May the light guide you both. Remember, your bond is your greatest strength. Trust in each other."

As they prepared to leave, Elara felt a mix of emotions—fear, hope, and a growing sense of purpose. The prophecy had given her a new perspective on her powers, turning what she had seen as a curse into a potential blessing. She squeezed Gareth's hand, grateful for his unwavering support.

"Are you ready?" Gareth asked, his voice gentle.

Elara nodded, her resolve firm. "Yes. Let's find the answers we need."

They stepped out of the hut, the forest around them seeming both familiar and ominous. The journey to the ruins would be challenging, but Elara felt a renewed sense of hope. With Gareth by her side and Brynn's guidance, she was ready to face whatever lay ahead.

The path ahead was fraught with unknown dangers, but it also held the promise of understanding and control. For the first time, Elara felt that she was moving towards her destiny, rather than being swept along by forces beyond her control.

As they walked deeper into the forest, the trees closing in around them, Elara looked up at Gareth. "Thank you for believing in me," she said softly.

Gareth smiled, his blue eyes warm. "We're in this together, Elara. No matter what."

Their bond, forged through adversity and shared purpose, would be tested in the trials to come. But with each step, they grew stronger, ready to face the challenges of their intertwined destinies.

Elder Brynn's hut was filled with the scent of burning herbs, casting a soothing atmosphere over the room. Elara and Gareth sat across from the old man, absorbing the weight of his words. The revelation of the prophecy had shifted their understanding of their mission entirely.

"Elara, your powers are not just a curse. They are a key," Brynn said, his voice steady. "A key to a greater destiny."

Elara looked at Brynn, her eyes wide with hope and fear. "But how can I control something so volatile? Every time I try, it ends in disaster."

Brynn nodded thoughtfully. "Control comes from understanding. We must delve into the origins of your powers. Do you know anything about your lineage?"

Elara shook her head. "My parents never spoke of it. They died when I was young."

The elder sighed. "Often, power of this magnitude is inherited. There may be answers in your family's past."

Gareth leaned forward, his expression serious. "We need to find those answers. Is there a place we can start?"

Brynn stroked his beard, contemplating. "There are ancient ruins in the deepest part of this forest. They hold secrets and might contain the knowledge you seek. But be warned, the journey is perilous."

Elara's determination hardened. "I don't care about the danger. I need to understand who I am and why this is happening."

Gareth nodded in agreement. "We'll face it together. Tell us more about these ruins."

Brynn's eyes darkened slightly. "The ruins are remnants of an ancient civilization that dabbled in powerful magic. They are protected by enchantments and creatures born of the shadows. But within, you may find texts or artifacts that reveal your heritage."

Elara glanced at Gareth, finding reassurance in his steady presence. "We have to go. This could be the key to everything."

Brynn rose and walked to a shelf, retrieving a small, intricately carved box. "Take this," he said, handing it to Gareth. "It's an amulet of protection. It will shield you from some of the dangers you will face."

Gareth accepted the amulet, slipping it over his head. "Thank you, Elder Brynn. We'll make sure it's put to good use."

Brynn smiled warmly. "May the light guide you both. Remember, your bond is your greatest strength. Trust in each other."

As they prepared to leave, Elara felt a mix of emotions—fear, hope, and a growing sense of purpose. The prophecy had given her a new perspective on her powers, turning what she had seen as a curse into a potential blessing. She squeezed Gareth's hand, grateful for his unwavering support.

"Are you ready?" Gareth asked, his voice gentle.

Elara nodded, her resolve firm. "Yes. Let's find the answers we need."

They stepped out of the hut, the forest around them seeming both familiar and ominous. The journey to the ruins would be challenging, but Elara felt a renewed sense of hope. With Gareth by her side and Brynn's guidance, she was ready to face whatever lay ahead.

The path ahead was fraught with unknown dangers, but it also held the promise of understanding and control. For the first time, Elara felt that she was moving towards her destiny, rather than being swept along by forces beyond her control.

As they walked deeper into the forest, the trees closing in around them, Elara looked up at Gareth. "Thank you for believing in me," she said softly.

Gareth smiled, his blue eyes warm. "We're in this together, Elara. No matter what."

Their bond, forged through adversity and shared purpose, would be tested in the trials to come. But with each step, they grew stronger, ready to face the challenges of their intertwined destinies.

The forest grew darker and more foreboding as Elara and Gareth ventured deeper, the path ahead obscured by thick foliage and twisted branches. The air was thick with the scent of damp earth and decaying leaves. Despite the oppressive atmosphere, a sense of resolve had settled over Elara. She was determined to uncover the truth about her powers and fulfill the prophecy that Elder Brynn had revealed.

"Do you think the ruins will really have the answers we need?" Elara asked, breaking the silence.

Gareth glanced at her, his expression thoughtful. "If Brynn believes it, then I trust his judgment. We have to explore every possibility."

Elara nodded, determination hardening her resolve. "I just want to understand why this is happening to me. Why I was cursed with these powers."

Gareth reached out, taking her hand in his. "You weren't cursed, Elara. You were chosen. There's a difference."

Elara looked at him, her eyes filled with uncertainty. "Chosen for what? To bring chaos and destruction?"

"To bring balance," Gareth said firmly. "And to fulfill a destiny greater than either of us can imagine."

They continued walking, the silence between them now comfortable. The forest seemed to close in around them, the trees whispering secrets and the shadows shifting with unseen movements. Elara could feel the presence of something ancient and powerful, a reminder of the magic that permeated the world.

After what felt like hours, they reached a clearing. In the center stood the ancient ruins, their stone walls covered in moss and ivy. The air was thick with the scent of magic, and Elara could feel the energy thrumming beneath her skin.

"This is it," Gareth said, his voice hushed with awe. "The answers we seek are inside."

Elara took a deep breath, steeling herself for what lay ahead. "Let's do this."

They approached the entrance, the heavy stone doors looming before them. Gareth placed his hand on the door, feeling the cool stone beneath his fingers. With a grunt of effort, he pushed the doors open, revealing a dark corridor that stretched into the depths of the ruins.

Elara hesitated, her fear threatening to overwhelm her. Gareth sensed her hesitation and squeezed her hand reassuringly. "We'll face whatever comes together," he said softly.

Elara nodded, drawing strength from his presence. "Together."

They stepped into the corridor, the air growing colder and the darkness more oppressive with each step. The walls were lined with ancient carvings, their meanings lost to time. Elara felt a strange sense of familiarity as she looked at the symbols, as if they were calling to something deep within her.

As they ventured deeper into the ruins, they reached a large chamber. In the center stood a stone pedestal, upon which rested a large, ornate book. The air crackled with energy, and Elara felt her powers stirring in response.

"This must be it," Gareth said, approaching the pedestal. "The knowledge we seek."

Elara stepped forward, her heart pounding. She reached out and touched the book, feeling a surge of power course through her. The symbols on the cover glowed faintly, responding to her touch.

"Open it," Gareth urged gently.

Elara nodded and carefully opened the book. The pages were filled with ancient text and intricate illustrations, depicting rituals and spells long forgotten. As she read, the words seemed to come alive, their meanings becoming clear.

"This is it," Elara whispered, her eyes wide with wonder. "The key to controlling my powers."

Gareth looked over her shoulder, his expression filled with awe. "We've found it, Elara. Now we can fulfill the prophecy."

Elara smiled, hope and determination shining in her eyes. "Yes. And together, we will restore balance to our worlds."

As they pored over the ancient text, a sense of purpose settled over them. They were no longer lost, no longer at the mercy of forces beyond their control. They had found the path forward, and with it, the hope of a brighter future.

Chapter 4
Trials of the Ruins

Elara and Gareth sat cross-legged on the cold stone floor of the ancient chamber, the flickering torchlight casting eerie shadows on the walls. The book lay open between them, its pages filled with cryptic symbols and illustrations that seemed to shift and change in the dim light.

"We need to decipher this," Gareth said, his voice a low murmur. "These symbols... they must hold the key to your powers."

Elara nodded, her fingers tracing the delicate lines of the ancient text. "It's like they're alive. I can feel the magic pulsing through them."

Gareth leaned closer, studying the page intently. "What does it say?"

Elara squinted, her brow furrowing in concentration. "It speaks of a ritual... one that requires a bond between two souls. A bond of trust and unity."

"A bond between us?" Gareth asked, his voice filled with curiosity and a hint of concern.

Elara nodded. "Yes. It says that our bond can channel the magic, control it. But we need to perform the ritual together."

Gareth looked at her, his blue eyes serious. "Are you sure about this, Elara? This kind of magic... it's powerful and dangerous."

"I have to try," Elara replied, determination hardening her voice. "I can't keep living in fear. If this is the only way to control my powers, then I have to do it."

Gareth placed a reassuring hand on her shoulder. "Then we do it together. What do we need for the ritual?"

Elara scanned the page, her fingers trembling slightly. "It requires a circle of protection, drawn with sacred herbs. We also need a chalice of pure water and a flame from a heartstone."

Gareth nodded. "We have the herbs and the chalice. But the heartstone... we'll need to find that."

Elara's eyes widened. "Heartstones are rare. They can only be found in the deepest parts of the forest."

"Then that's where we go," Gareth said resolutely. "We'll find the heartstone and perform the ritual. Together."

As they gathered their supplies, Elara felt a mixture of fear and excitement. The journey ahead would be perilous, but she felt a renewed sense of hope. With Gareth by her side, she believed they could overcome any obstacle.

"Ready?" Gareth asked, his voice steady and calm.

Elara took a deep breath, nodding. "Ready."

They left the ancient chamber and ventured deeper into the forest, the trees growing denser and the air growing colder with each step. The path was treacherous, but their determination drove them forward.

As they walked, Gareth broke the silence. "Elara, tell me more about your parents. What were they like?"

Elara's expression softened, a wistful smile playing on her lips. "They were kind and loving. My mother had a gentle spirit, always nurturing and supportive. My father was strong and protective, always making sure we were safe."

"And your powers?" Gareth asked gently. "Did they know about them?"

Elara nodded. "Yes. They tried to help me control them, but it was too difficult. They were afraid for me, but they never stopped loving me."

Gareth squeezed her hand. "I'm sorry you lost them. But you have their strength and love inside you. That's what makes you strong."

Elara felt a tear slip down her cheek, but she smiled through it. "Thank you, Gareth. That means a lot to me."

As they continued their journey, the bond between them grew stronger, forged through shared purpose and mutual trust. They were no longer just two individuals; they were a team, united in their quest to understand and control Elara's powers.

The forest grew darker and more oppressive as they ventured further, the thick canopy above blocking out most of the light. Strange sounds echoed around them, and the air was filled with a sense of foreboding. Despite the fear that gnawed at the edges of her mind, Elara felt a strong sense of resolve. She knew that finding the heartstone was crucial to their mission.

"We're getting close," Gareth said, his voice a low whisper. "I can feel it."

Elara nodded, her eyes scanning the dense underbrush. "The heartstone should be near a source of pure magic. Look for any signs of ancient enchantments."

As they searched, Gareth kept the conversation going, sensing that it helped keep Elara's fear at bay. "Do you remember the first time you felt your powers?"

Elara paused, her eyes distant. "Yes. I was very young, maybe five or six. I was playing in the garden, and I got upset because I couldn't reach a flower I wanted. Suddenly, the flower burst into flames. My parents rushed out, trying to calm me down. I was terrified."

Gareth nodded, understanding. "It must have been frightening, not knowing what was happening."

"It was," Elara admitted. "But my parents were always there for me. They tried to teach me control, but it was hard. The fear of hurting someone always made it worse."

Gareth's expression softened. "And now, you're facing that fear head-on. That's incredibly brave, Elara."

Before she could respond, a faint glow caught her eye. "Gareth, look over there!"

They moved cautiously towards the light, pushing aside branches and vines. In a small clearing, they found a shimmering pool of water, its surface glowing with an ethereal light. At the center of the pool, embedded in a stone pedestal, was the heartstone.

"That's it," Elara whispered, awe in her voice. "The heartstone."

Gareth approached the pedestal, examining the stone. "It's beautiful. But how do we get it out?"

Elara stepped closer, feeling the magic thrumming through the air. "The book mentioned a chant. I think I can do it."

Gareth stood beside her, offering silent support as Elara began to chant in the ancient language she had learned from the book. Her voice was steady, growing stronger with each word. The heartstone began to pulse in response, its glow intensifying.

As the chant reached its climax, the stone lifted from the pedestal, floating towards Elara. She reached out, her hands trembling slightly, and took the stone. The moment she touched it, a wave of energy surged through her, almost overwhelming in its intensity.

Gareth steadied her, his hands on her shoulders. "Are you alright?"

Elara nodded, her eyes wide with wonder. "Yes. I can feel its power. It's like it was meant for me."

Gareth smiled, relief evident on his face. "We did it. We have everything we need for the ritual."

Elara looked at him, gratitude and determination in her eyes. "Thank you, Gareth. For everything."

"We're in this together," Gareth reminded her. "Now, let's head back and perform the ritual. It's time to take control of your destiny."

As they made their way back through the forest, the heartstone's glow lighting their path, Elara felt a sense of hope she hadn't felt in years. With Gareth by her side and the heartstone in her hands, she believed they could overcome any challenge that lay ahead.

Back at Elder Brynn's hut, the air was charged with anticipation. The heartstone's glow filled the small space, casting dancing shadows on the walls. Gareth and Elara set to work, carefully following the instructions from the ancient book to prepare for the ritual that would help Elara control her powers.

Elder Brynn watched them with a keen eye, occasionally offering guidance. "Remember, the circle must be perfect. Any break in it could disrupt the flow of magic."

Gareth nodded, meticulously arranging the sacred herbs in a precise circle around Elara. "We've come this far. We can't afford any mistakes now."

Elara stood in the center of the circle, holding the heartstone. The energy emanating from it was both comforting and overwhelming. She took deep, steadying breaths, focusing on the task ahead.

"Elara," Elder Brynn said softly, "your connection with Gareth will be your anchor. Trust in him, and in yourself."

Elara glanced at Gareth, who gave her an encouraging smile. "We've got this, Elara. I'm right here with you."

With the preparations complete, Brynn handed Gareth the chalice filled with pure water. "Pour this at the center of the circle when Elara begins the incantation. It will activate the protective barrier."

Gareth took the chalice, his grip firm. "Understood."

Elara closed her eyes, centering herself. She began to chant, her voice clear and resonant. The ancient words flowed from her lips, filling the room with a powerful vibration. Gareth carefully poured the water at her feet, and a shimmering barrier sprang up around her.

The heartstone's glow intensified, bathing Elara in its light. She felt a surge of energy, stronger than anything she had ever experienced. It was as if the heartstone was merging with her, its power becoming her own.

Gareth watched in awe, his heart pounding. He could see the strain on Elara's face but also the determination. He reached out, his voice steady. "Stay with it, Elara. You can do this."

Elara's chant grew louder, the magic within her building to a crescendo. The heartstone pulsed in her hands, and she felt a profound connection with it, a sense of unity and purpose. As the final words left her lips, a brilliant flash of light filled the room.

When the light faded, Elara stood there, breathing heavily but with a new sense of calm. She opened her eyes, which now glowed with a controlled power. She looked at Gareth and Elder Brynn, a smile of relief spreading across her face.

"I did it," she whispered. "I can feel it. The control."

Gareth stepped into the circle, taking her hands in his. "You were incredible, Elara. I knew you could do it."

Elder Brynn nodded, his eyes twinkling with approval. "You have taken the first step, Elara. But remember, this is just the beginning. Mastery will come with time and practice."

Elara squeezed Gareth's hands, her eyes filled with gratitude. "Thank you, both of you. I couldn't have done this without you."

As they celebrated the success of the ritual, a sudden chill filled the room. The torches flickered, and the air grew heavy with an oppressive energy. Elara's newfound control was about to be tested in ways she had never imagined.

A dark figure materialized in the corner of the hut, its presence commanding and terrifying. The Shadow King had arrived, his eyes glowing with malevolent intent.

"Elara," he intoned, his voice echoing with dark power. "You have done well to reach this point. But do not think for a moment that you are beyond my reach."

Gareth instinctively stepped in front of Elara, his sword drawn. "What do you want, Shadow King? Leave her alone."

The Shadow King laughed, a sound that sent shivers down their spines. "Brave knight, you cannot protect her forever. She is bound to me, just as you are bound to her."

Elara felt a surge of fear but quickly steadied herself, drawing on the strength of the heartstone. "I am not afraid of you," she said, her voice firm. "I will not let you control me."

The Shadow King's eyes narrowed. "Such defiance. It will be your undoing. You think you can control the darkness within you? You have no idea of the power you wield."

Elder Brynn stepped forward, his face resolute. "She is not alone, Shadow King. We stand with her."

The Shadow King sneered. "Fools, all of you. You meddle in forces beyond your comprehension. The bond you share," he pointed at Elara and Gareth, "is strong, but it will not save you from what is to come."

Gareth tightened his grip on his sword. "We will face whatever comes together. Your threats mean nothing."

A dark energy began to swirl around the Shadow King, his form growing more imposing. "Very well. If it is a fight you seek, a fight you shall have."

Elara stepped forward, her eyes blazing with determination. "No. This ends now."

She raised the heartstone, channeling its power through her. The room filled with a brilliant light, pushing back the shadows. The Shadow King roared in fury, his form flickering and weakening under the onslaught of Elara's magic.

"You cannot defeat me!" he screamed, his voice a blend of rage and desperation.

Elara's voice was steady and strong. "I can, and I will. You have no power over me."

With a final, blinding flash, the Shadow King's presence was banished from the hut. The oppressive energy dissipated, leaving the room filled with an almost serene silence.

Gareth sheathed his sword, looking at Elara with admiration and relief. "You did it, Elara. You drove him away."

Elder Brynn nodded, his expression thoughtful. "But he will return. The Shadow King is relentless. We must be prepared for whatever comes next."

Elara took a deep breath, feeling the weight of their words. "We will be ready. Together, we can face anything."

The three of them stood in the quiet hut, united in their resolve. The journey ahead would be fraught with challenges, but Elara knew that with Gareth and Brynn by her side, she could overcome any obstacle. She had found her strength, and with it, the hope of a brighter future.

Chapter 5
Rising Tensions

The atmosphere in Elder Brynn's hut was thick with tension. The confrontation with the Shadow King had left an indelible mark on all three of them. Elara, Gareth, and Brynn sat in the dim light, the silence punctuated only by the crackling of the fire.

Elara looked down at the heartstone in her hands, its glow subdued now. "I can't believe he came here," she said quietly, breaking the silence. "What if he comes back?"

Gareth's expression was resolute. "We'll be ready for him. We've faced him once, and we can do it again."

Brynn nodded, but his eyes were shadowed with concern. "The Shadow King will not give up easily. He is determined to break you, Elara. You must be prepared for the trials ahead."

Elara felt a shiver run down her spine. "But how? How can we possibly prepare for something like that?"

Brynn leaned forward, his gaze intense. "By understanding your powers more deeply and by strengthening the bond between you and Gareth. This bond is your greatest weapon against the Shadow King."

Gareth took Elara's hand, his grip reassuring. "We'll train together, learn more about our connection and how to use it. We won't let him win."

Elara nodded, drawing strength from Gareth's confidence. "Alright. Let's start right away. We can't afford to waste any time."

As they began their preparations, a sense of determination settled over them. The encounter with the Shadow King had been a harsh reminder of the dangers they faced, but it had also solidified their resolve to fight back.

The days that followed were filled with intense training. Elara and Gareth worked tirelessly, guided by Elder Brynn's wisdom. They practiced controlling Elara's powers, focusing on harnessing the energy without letting it overwhelm her. But more importantly, they worked on strengthening the bond between them, learning to trust and support each other in new ways.

One evening, as the sun dipped below the horizon, casting long shadows over the forest, Elara and Gareth sat together near the edge of the clearing. The day's training had been particularly grueling, and both of them were exhausted.

Elara looked at Gareth, her eyes reflecting the fading light. "Do you ever doubt, Gareth? Do you ever think we won't be able to do this?"

Gareth shook his head, his expression steadfast. "No, Elara. I believe in you. I believe in us. We've come so far already. We can't turn back now."

Elara sighed, a mixture of fatigue and gratitude in her voice. "I don't know what I'd do without you. You're my rock, Gareth."

Gareth smiled, his blue eyes warm. "And you're my strength. Together, we're unstoppable."

They fell into a comfortable silence, the bond between them growing stronger with each passing moment. Elara could feel the connection, a palpable force that linked their souls. It was this bond that gave her the courage to face whatever lay ahead.

"Do you remember the first time we met?" Elara asked suddenly, a hint of a smile playing on her lips.

Gareth chuckled. "How could I forget? You were so wary of me. I thought for sure you were going to send me away."

Elara laughed softly. "I didn't know what to think. You were this mysterious knight from the shadow realm, sent to kill me. It seemed too crazy to be real."

"And now look at us," Gareth said, his voice filled with wonder. "We've faced the Shadow King together. We've found a way to control your powers. We're stronger than ever."

Elara nodded, her eyes shining with determination. "Yes, we are. And we'll keep getting stronger. No matter what."

Their conversation was interrupted by the sound of footsteps. Elder Brynn approached, his face etched with concern. "I've been sensing a disturbance in the magic around us," he said, his voice low. "The Shadow King is not giving up. He's gathering his forces."

Elara's heart sank. "What do we do?"

Brynn looked at them both, his eyes filled with a fierce determination. "We prepare for battle. We strengthen our defenses and rally the villagers. This fight is not just yours, Elara. It's all of ours."

Gareth stood up, his expression resolute. "We'll stand together. We'll protect our home and each other."

Elara rose to her feet, her fear replaced by a burning resolve. "Yes. We'll fight. And we'll win."

As the night fell, the three of them worked tirelessly, preparing for the coming battle. The bond between Elara and Gareth was now a powerful force, a beacon of hope in the encroaching darkness. They were ready to face whatever the Shadow King would throw at them, united in their purpose and strengthened by their love.

The battle ahead would be the greatest challenge they had ever faced, but they were no longer afraid. Together, they were unstoppable.

As dawn broke over the village, a sense of urgency permeated the air. The villagers, long accustomed to living in fear of the shadow realm, now felt a glimmer of hope. Word had spread of Elara's newfound control over her powers and the alliance she had formed with Gareth and Elder Brynn. The time had come to rally the villagers and prepare them for the impending battle.

In the village square, Elara stood beside Gareth and Elder Brynn, her heart pounding with a mix of anxiety and determination. The villagers gathered around, their faces a mixture of curiosity and apprehension.

"Thank you for coming," Elara began, her voice strong despite the nervousness she felt. "We are all aware of the growing threat from the shadow realm. The Shadow King will not stop until he has conquered our world."

Murmurs rippled through the crowd, the fear in their eyes palpable.

"But we are not powerless," Gareth interjected, stepping forward. "Elara has learned to control her powers, and together we have the strength to stand against the Shadow King. We must unite and fight to protect our home."

An elderly villager, Thomas, stepped forward. "How can we, ordinary villagers, fight against such darkness?"

Elara met his gaze, her eyes filled with resolve. "By standing together. Each of you has a role to play. We need everyone's help to fortify our defenses and prepare for the battle ahead."

A young woman, clutching her child, spoke up. "What can we do? We're not warriors."

Elder Brynn raised his hand, his voice calm and authoritative. "There is strength in unity. We will train those who can fight and prepare those who cannot to support in other ways. Every effort counts."

A sense of determination began to replace the fear in the villagers' eyes. They looked at Elara, Gareth, and Brynn, drawing courage from their unwavering resolve.

"We will fight," Thomas said, his voice steady. "For our families, for our home."

Other villagers nodded in agreement, their faces hardening with resolve.

Gareth smiled, his heart swelling with pride. "Thank you. Together, we will show the Shadow King that we will not be easily defeated."

The villagers dispersed, the square buzzing with activity as they began to prepare. Elara and Gareth moved through the crowd, offering words of encouragement and instruction. The once fearful village was now a hive of determined activity, united by a common goal.

Elara stopped to help a group of villagers weaving protective charms. "These will help shield us from the Shadow King's dark magic," she explained, her hands deftly tying the intricate knots.

Gareth joined a group of men sharpening weapons. "We need to be ready for close combat," he said, demonstrating how to hold the sword. "Stay strong and stay together."

Elder Brynn coordinated the efforts, his presence a calming influence amidst the chaos. "Remember, every action you take now strengthens our chances. We must be diligent and focused."

As the day wore on, the village transformed. Barricades were erected, weapons were distributed, and the air was filled with the hum of preparation. The villagers, once driven by fear, now worked with a sense of purpose and determination.

Elara stood back, watching the transformation with a mixture of pride and hope. She felt Gareth's presence beside her, his hand gently resting on her shoulder.

"We're ready," she said softly, her eyes meeting his.

Gareth nodded, his expression serious. "Yes, we are. And whatever happens, we'll face it together."

As night fell, the village quieted. The preparations were complete, and a tense calm settled over the villagers. They gathered in small groups, sharing quiet conversations and bolstering each other's spirits.

Elara and Gareth walked through the village, checking on the fortifications and offering final words of encouragement. The weight of what was to come pressed heavily on them, but their bond remained a source of strength.

Near the edge of the village, they found Elder Brynn speaking with a group of villagers. He looked up as they approached, his eyes filled with a quiet resolve. “Everything is in place,” he said. “Now we wait.”

Elara nodded, taking a deep breath. “Thank you, Brynn. For everything.”

Brynn smiled warmly. “It is my honor to stand with you. Remember, you are stronger than you know.”

As they moved away, Elara felt a surge of emotion. “I’m scared, Gareth,” she admitted, her voice barely above a whisper.

Gareth stopped and turned to face her, his hands resting gently on her shoulders. “It’s okay to be scared. But remember, you’re not alone. We’re all in this together.”

Elara nodded, drawing strength from his unwavering gaze. “I know. And I’m ready to fight for our home.”

Gareth smiled, his eyes reflecting the flickering torchlight. “So am I.”

They continued their walk, the village now bathed in the soft glow of moonlight. The calm before the storm was palpable, each moment stretching out as they waited for the inevitable.

As they reached the center of the village, Elara looked up at the night sky, the stars shining brightly. “We will win, Gareth. We have to.”

Gareth followed her gaze, his hand slipping into hers. “We will. Together.”

In the stillness of the night, surrounded by the strength of their community and the bond they shared, Elara and Gareth prepared to face the coming battle with hope and determination. The challenges ahead would be great, but their resolve was unbreakable.

Chapter 6
The Battle Begins

The air was still, the village wrapped in a cloak of uneasy silence. The moon hung high in the sky, casting an ethereal glow over the fortified barricades and the determined faces of the villagers. They stood ready, their weapons at hand, eyes scanning the darkness for any sign of movement.

Elara stood at the front line, the heartstone glowing faintly at her chest. She could feel its power thrumming through her veins, a steady reminder of the strength she now possessed. Beside her, Gareth held his sword, his expression a mask of steely resolve.

"We've done everything we can to prepare," Gareth said, his voice low and steady. "Now, we wait."

Elara nodded, her eyes never leaving the forest edge. "Whatever happens, we stand together."

As the night deepened, a chill settled over the village. The tension was palpable, each villager standing at the ready, hearts pounding in unison. Suddenly, a distant rustling broke the silence. Shadows flickered at the edge of the forest, growing larger and more distinct as they moved closer.

Elara tightened her grip on the heartstone, feeling its energy respond to her anxiety. "They're coming."

Gareth raised his sword, his voice calm but commanding. "Hold your positions! Remember your training!"

The first wave of shadow creatures emerged from the darkness, their forms twisted and grotesque. They moved with unnatural speed, eyes glowing with malevolence. The villagers held their ground, weapons at the ready.

"Steady!" Elara called out, her voice clear and strong. "Wait for my signal!"

The creatures advanced, their snarls filling the air. Elara felt the power of the heartstone surge within her, and she raised her hand, channeling its energy. A beam of light shot from her palm, striking the nearest creature and disintegrating it instantly.

"Now!" she shouted, unleashing another blast of energy.

The villagers sprang into action, meeting the creatures with a fierce determination. Swords clashed, arrows flew, and spells were cast, each villager fighting with a strength born of desperation and hope.

Elara moved through the chaos, her power flowing freely as she struck down one creature after another. She could see Gareth in the thick of the battle, his sword flashing as he fought with skill and precision. They worked in tandem, their bond guiding their movements and amplifying their strength.

Despite their efforts, the shadow creatures kept coming, an endless tide of darkness. The villagers fought valiantly, but the strain was beginning to show. Elara knew they couldn't hold out forever.

"We need to break their ranks!" Gareth shouted, his voice cutting through the din of battle. "Elara, can you create a barrier?"

Elara nodded, her mind racing. "I'll try."

She focused her energy, drawing on the heartstone's power. With a fierce concentration, she extended her hands, forming a shimmering barrier of light. The creatures recoiled, hissing in fury as they slammed against the barrier, unable to penetrate it.

"Hold it as long as you can!" Gareth urged, rallying the villagers. "We need to regroup!"

Elara gritted her teeth, the effort of maintaining the barrier draining her strength. She could feel the strain, but she refused to give in. "Hurry, Gareth," she whispered, her voice strained. "I can't hold it much longer."

Gareth nodded, his eyes meeting hers. “You’re doing great, Elara. Just a little longer.”

With the barrier in place, the villagers quickly regrouped, tending to the wounded and reinforcing their defenses. The brief respite gave them a chance to catch their breath and prepare for the next wave.

“Elara,” Gareth said, placing a reassuring hand on her shoulder. “You’re incredible. We wouldn’t have made it this far without you.”

Elara managed a weary smile, her body trembling from the effort. “We’re not done yet, Gareth. But we’re ready for whatever comes next.”

The respite was short-lived. As the villagers regrouped, a deeper, more ominous darkness began to gather at the edge of the forest. The air grew colder, and an unnatural silence fell over the battlefield. Elara felt a chill run down her spine. She knew this was just the beginning.

“We need to stay vigilant,” Elder Brynn said, his eyes scanning the horizon. “The Shadow King is not finished.”

As if on cue, the ground trembled beneath their feet. From the depths of the forest, the Shadow King emerged, his form towering and cloaked in darkness. His eyes glowed with a malevolent light, and a sinister smile played on his lips.

“Elara,” he called, his voice echoing through the night. “You cannot hide from me. Your power belongs to me.”

Gareth stepped forward, his sword raised defiantly. “We will not let you take her. She is stronger than you think.”

The Shadow King laughed, a sound that sent shivers through the villagers. “You think you can defy me? You are mere mortals, nothing more.”

Elara felt the weight of his gaze, but she stood her ground. “We are stronger together. You will not win.”

The Shadow King's eyes narrowed. "We shall see."

With a wave of his hand, he summoned a horde of shadow creatures, their forms more terrifying than before. They surged forward, crashing against the villagers' defenses. The battle resumed with renewed ferocity.

Gareth fought at Elara's side, their movements synchronized. "We need to take him down, Elara. He's the source of their power."

Elara nodded, determination hardening her resolve. "I'll focus on the creatures. You go for him."

Gareth hesitated, his eyes filled with concern. "Are you sure?"

"Yes," Elara replied, her voice steady. "I can handle this. Go."

Gareth gave her a nod, then charged toward the Shadow King, his sword gleaming in the moonlight. Elara turned her attention to the creatures, her hands glowing with the heartstone's energy. She unleashed a barrage of light, striking down the creatures one by one.

As Gareth closed in on the Shadow King, the dark lord's eyes gleamed with amusement. "You dare challenge me, knight?"

Gareth's grip tightened on his sword. "I do. For Elara, and for our world."

The Shadow King raised his hand, summoning dark tendrils that lashed out at Gareth. He dodged and parried, his movements swift and precise. "You cannot win," the Shadow King sneered. "You are outmatched."

Gareth's eyes blazed with determination. "We'll see about that."

He struck with all his might, his sword clashing against the Shadow King's dark shield. The force of the impact sent shockwaves through the air. Elara could see the strain on Gareth's face, but he fought on, relentless.

Meanwhile, Elara continued to hold back the creatures, her energy waning. She could feel the heartstone's power dimming, and she knew she had to act fast. "Gareth," she called out, her voice carrying through the chaos. "I need your help!"

Gareth glanced back at her, his expression torn. "I can't leave you alone!"

"You won't," Elara said, her voice filled with resolve. "We need to do this together. Trust me."

Gareth nodded, his trust in her unwavering. He broke away from the Shadow King, fighting his way back to Elara's side. "What do you need?"

Elara's eyes met his, a plan forming in her mind. "We need to combine our powers. Together, we can defeat him."

Gareth took her hand, their bond strengthening their resolve. "Let's do it."

They turned to face the Shadow King, their hands glowing with combined energy. Elara could feel the heartstone's power merging with Gareth's strength, creating a force unlike anything she had ever felt.

The Shadow King's eyes widened in surprise. "What are you doing?"

Elara's voice was steady, filled with determination. "Ending this."

Together, they unleashed a blast of light and energy, their combined power surging toward the Shadow King. The darkness around him shattered, and he let out a roar of fury and pain. The villagers watched in awe as the light enveloped the Shadow King, consuming him in a brilliant blaze.

When the light faded, the Shadow King was gone, his darkness vanquished. The shadow creatures dissolved into nothingness, their hold over the village broken.

Elara and Gareth stood together, their hands still joined, their hearts pounding with the realization of their victory. The villagers erupted in cheers, their voices filled with joy and relief.

Elder Brynn approached them, his eyes shining with pride. "You did it. You saved us all."

Elara smiled, her eyes meeting Gareth's. "We did it together."

Gareth squeezed her hand, his voice filled with emotion. "Together."

As the first light of dawn broke over the horizon, the village began to heal, its people united by the bond they had forged in the face of darkness. Elara and Gareth knew that their journey was far from over, but they faced the future with hope and strength, ready for whatever challenges lay ahead.

As the last of the shadow creatures dissolved into the night, a profound silence settled over the battlefield. The villagers, breathless and weary, began to realize the magnitude of their victory. The air, once heavy with fear and anticipation, now carried a sense of relief and triumph.

Elara stood at the center of the village square, her chest heaving with exertion. The heartstone, now dimmed, hung around her neck, a testament to the power she had wielded. She looked around at the faces of her fellow villagers, seeing the same mixture of exhaustion and elation mirrored in their expressions.

Gareth approached her, his sword sheathed but his eyes still sharp and alert. "Elara, are you alright?"

Elara nodded, a tired but genuine smile spreading across her face. "I'm fine, Gareth. We did it. We really did it."

Gareth took her hand, squeezing it gently. "You were incredible. The way you controlled your power... it was like nothing I've ever seen."

Elara felt a surge of warmth at his words. "I couldn't have done it without you. Your strength, your support... it made all the difference."

Elder Brynn joined them, his wise eyes filled with pride. "You both have shown remarkable courage and resilience. The bond you share has truly become your greatest weapon."

The villagers began to gather around them, expressions of gratitude and admiration on their faces. Thomas, the elderly villager who had initially questioned their ability to fight, stepped forward. "Elara, Gareth, you have saved us all. We owe you our lives."

Elara shook her head, her voice humble. "We did this together. Every single one of you played a part in this victory."

A young girl approached, holding a small bouquet of wildflowers. She shyly handed them to Elara, her eyes wide with admiration. "Thank you, Elara. You're a hero."

Elara accepted the flowers, tears of gratitude welling in her eyes. "Thank you. But remember, true heroes are those who stand up for each other, just like all of you did tonight."

As the villagers began to tend to the wounded and rebuild their defenses, a sense of unity and hope settled over the village. The battle had been won, but they knew their journey was far from over.

As the night wore on, Elara and Gareth found a moment of peace by the village well. The moon cast a gentle glow over the scene, and the distant sounds of the villagers slowly winding down filled the air. They sat side by side, their hands still intertwined, the weight of the night's events beginning to sink in.

"Elara," Gareth began, his voice soft and filled with emotion, "I've never felt a bond like this before. What we did tonight... it was beyond anything I could have imagined."

Elara looked at him, her eyes reflecting the same depth of feeling. "I know, Gareth. It's like our souls are connected. I can feel your strength, your resolve. It gives me hope."

Gareth turned to face her fully, his expression earnest. "You are the bravest person I've ever known. The way you stood up to the Shadow King, the way you protected our people... I'm in awe of you."

Elara blushed slightly, her heart swelling with affection. "I couldn't have done it without you. You believed in me when I didn't believe in myself. You gave me the courage to fight."

Gareth's eyes softened, and he gently cupped her face in his hands. "Elara, you are my light in the darkness. Together, we can face anything."

Elara felt tears prick at the corners of her eyes, but they were tears of joy and gratitude. "Gareth, I... I feel the same way. You've been my rock, my protector. I'm so grateful for you."

Their faces were close, the world around them fading into the background. In that moment, everything else seemed to disappear. Gareth leaned in, and their lips met in a tender, heartfelt kiss. It was a kiss filled with the promise of a future together, a future where they would continue to fight side by side.

When they finally pulled apart, they remained close, foreheads touching. "We should get some rest," Gareth said gently. "Tomorrow will bring new challenges."

Elara nodded, her eyes still closed, savoring the warmth of the moment. "Yes, we need to be ready. But for now, I'm just glad we have each other."

They stood up, still holding hands, and made their way back to the center of the village. The villagers were already beginning to gather, their faces lit with hope and determination. They knew that the Shadow King was not gone for good, but they also knew that with Elara and Gareth leading them, they had a fighting chance.

Elder Brynn met them with a knowing smile. "Rest well, both of you. Tomorrow, we continue our journey. But tonight, we celebrate our victory."

As the first light of dawn began to break over the horizon, Elara and Gareth found a place to rest, their hands still intertwined. They knew that their journey was far from over, but they also knew that together, they could face whatever challenges lay ahead.

In the quiet moments before sleep claimed them, Elara whispered, "Thank you, Gareth. For everything."

Gareth smiled, his thumb gently caressing the back of her hand. "Always, Elara. Always."

As they drifted off to sleep, the village around them slowly came to life, ready to face a new day with renewed strength and hope. The bond between Elara and Gareth had not only saved their village but had also given them the courage to continue their fight against the darkness, together.

Chapter 7
New Allies and Old Foes

The morning sun filtered through the trees, casting a warm glow over the village square where the villagers had gathered. The atmosphere was charged with a mix of hope and apprehension as they prepared for the challenges ahead. Elara and Gareth stood at the center, ready to address the crowd.

Elder Brynn raised his hand, calling for silence. "Our victory last night was a significant one, but the Shadow King will not rest. We must prepare for his return. Today, we form our strategy."

Thomas, the elder villager, stepped forward. "How can we be sure he won't attack again soon? We need a plan."

Gareth nodded. "We will strengthen our defenses and train everyone who can fight. But we also need to find allies. There are other villages, other realms, that face the same threat. If we unite, we stand a better chance."

A murmur of agreement rippled through the crowd. Elara stepped forward, her voice steady. "We must also seek out those with knowledge of the Shadow King's weaknesses. Elder Brynn has already provided invaluable insight, but there may be others who can help."

Lila, one of Elara's closest friends, spoke up. "What about the Guardians of the Sacred Grove? They are known for their ancient wisdom and powerful magic."

Brynn nodded thoughtfully. "The Guardians could indeed be powerful allies. Reaching them, however, will be a perilous journey. They reside deep within the Enchanted Forest, protected by enchantments and creatures of legend."

Gareth's eyes met Elara's. "We need to go. The Guardians might hold the key to defeating the Shadow King once and for all."

Elara nodded, determination in her gaze. "We'll leave at first light. In the meantime, we need to ensure the village is as fortified as possible."

Thomas stepped forward again. "What can the rest of us do? We're not all fighters."

Gareth smiled reassuringly. "Everyone has a role. We need crafters to repair and reinforce our defenses, scouts to keep watch, and healers to tend to the wounded. Every effort counts."

The villagers nodded, a renewed sense of purpose filling the air. They began to disperse, each person heading to their assigned tasks. Elara and Gareth stood with Elder Brynn, discussing the details of their journey.

"We'll need supplies and a map of the Enchanted Forest," Gareth said. "Do we have anyone who's traveled there before?"

Brynn shook his head. "The forest is treacherous, and few dare to venture into its depths. But I can provide you with what knowledge I have. Be wary of the forest's tricks. It is alive and will test you."

Elara took a deep breath. "We've faced many challenges already. We'll get through this one, too. For the sake of the village and for our future."

Brynn placed a hand on her shoulder. "Your strength and courage are inspiring, Elara. Trust in each other and in the bond you share. It will guide you through the darkest of times."

Gareth squeezed Elara's hand. "We'll be back with the Guardians' help. Until then, stay strong."

As they prepared for their journey, the village buzzed with activity. Defenses were reinforced, and supplies were gathered. Elara and Gareth shared a quiet moment, the weight of their mission settling over them.

"We're ready for this," Gareth said, his voice filled with conviction. "Together, we can face anything."

Elara nodded, her eyes shining with determination. "Together."

At dawn, Elara and Gareth set out, the villagers sending them off with hopeful smiles and silent prayers. The path to the Enchanted Forest was long and winding, the terrain becoming more treacherous with each step. The air grew cooler, and the trees more dense, their branches forming a canopy that blocked out the sunlight.

As they walked, Gareth glanced at Elara. "Are you alright? This journey won't be easy."

Elara smiled, though her eyes were shadowed with worry. "I'm fine. It's just... the unknown. The forest, the Guardians... I've only heard stories."

Gareth nodded. "I understand. But we've faced worse. And we're not alone. We have each other."

Elara squeezed his hand. "I know. And that makes all the difference."

They continued in silence, the forest growing darker and more mysterious. Strange sounds echoed around them, and they could feel the forest watching their every move. The air was thick with magic, and every step felt like a test.

"Do you think the Guardians will help us?" Elara asked, breaking the silence.

Gareth looked thoughtful. "They value wisdom and strength. If we prove ourselves worthy, they might. But we must be prepared for anything."

Elara nodded, her resolve hardening. "We'll do whatever it takes. For the village, for our people."

As they ventured deeper, they encountered the first of the forest's challenges. A dense fog rolled in, obscuring their path. The trees seemed to shift and move, creating an ever-changing maze.

"We need to stay close," Gareth said, his voice steady. "Don't let the forest separate us."

Elara nodded, gripping his hand tightly. "I won't. We'll get through this."

They navigated the maze, their bond guiding them through the fog. At times, the whispers of the forest seemed to taunt them, but they pressed on, their determination unwavering.

Finally, the fog lifted, revealing a clearing bathed in a soft, otherworldly light. At the center stood a group of figures, their forms glowing with a gentle, ethereal glow. The Guardians of the Sacred Grove.

Elara and Gareth approached cautiously, their hearts pounding. The lead Guardian, a tall figure with eyes like liquid silver, stepped forward.

"Who seeks the wisdom of the Guardians?" the Guardian asked, their voice a melodic echo.

Elara bowed her head respectfully. "I am Elara, and this is Gareth. We seek your help to defeat the Shadow King and protect our village."

The Guardian studied them for a moment, their gaze piercing. "You carry the heartstone, Elara. Its power is great, but it is your bond that is truly remarkable. Why should we help you?"

Gareth stepped forward, his voice strong and clear. "Because we fight for more than just ourselves. We fight for our people, for hope, and for a future free from darkness. Help us, and we can make a difference."

The Guardians exchanged glances, their expressions unreadable. Finally, the lead Guardian nodded. "Very well. We will help you. But know this: the path ahead is fraught with danger and sacrifice. Are you prepared?"

Elara and Gareth exchanged a determined glance. "We are prepared," Elara said firmly. "We'll do whatever it takes."

The Guardian smiled, a rare and beautiful sight. "Then let us begin. Together, we will face the darkness and emerge victorious."

The ethereal glow of the Guardians illuminated the clearing, casting long shadows that danced like whispers in the twilight. Elara and Gareth stood before them, hearts pounding with a mixture of anticipation and determination. The lead Guardian, with eyes like liquid silver, studied them intently.

"You seek to defeat the Shadow King," the Guardian intoned, their voice a harmonious blend of power and serenity. "But such a task requires more than just bravery. It requires understanding and unity."

Elara stepped forward, her voice steady despite the weight of the moment. "We've come to learn, to seek your wisdom. We know that alone we are not enough, but together, with your guidance, we believe we can succeed."

The Guardian nodded, a faint smile playing on their lips. "Your bond is strong. This will be your greatest strength. But there are trials you must face to harness the true power within you."

Gareth tightened his grip on Elara's hand. "We're ready. Whatever it takes, we'll face it together."

A younger Guardian, their eyes a deep forest green, spoke up. "The first trial will test your unity. Follow me."

The Guardian led them to a secluded part of the grove, where ancient trees formed a natural circle. In the center lay a crystal-clear pool, its surface shimmering with magical energy.

"This is the Pool of Reflection," the young Guardian explained. "Look into it and confront the truths it reveals. Only by facing your deepest fears and doubts can you strengthen your bond."

Elara and Gareth approached the pool, their reflections wavering on the surface. Elara took a deep breath and knelt beside it, Gareth following suit.

"Elara," Gareth said softly, his eyes locked on hers. "No matter what we see, remember we're in this together."

Elara nodded, her heart swelling with gratitude. "Together."

As they gazed into the pool, the water began to swirl, their reflections morphing into scenes from their past and potential futures. Elara saw herself as a young girl, struggling with her uncontrollable powers, isolated and afraid. She saw the villagers' fear and mistrust, and the weight of their expectations.

Gareth's reflection showed him as a lone knight, battling shadows with no one to rely on, his face etched with loneliness and duty. He saw the pain of losing comrades and the burden of responsibility.

"Elara," the vision of young Gareth spoke, his voice tinged with sorrow. "Do you ever fear that you won't be able to control your powers? That you might hurt those you love?"

Elara's eyes filled with tears, the weight of her fears laid bare. "Yes, I do. Every day. But with you, I've found hope and strength. I'm no longer alone."

The vision shifted, showing them a future where they stood together, facing the Shadow King. They were surrounded by darkness, but their bond shone like a beacon, unwavering and strong.

"Gareth," the vision of future Elara said, her voice filled with determination. "Do you trust that we can overcome this together?"

Gareth's reflection looked at Elara with unwavering faith. "I trust you with my life. Together, we're unstoppable."

The pool's surface stilled, their reflections returning to normal. Elara and Gareth looked at each other, their connection deeper and more profound.

"You have faced your fears and doubts," the young Guardian said, their voice filled with respect. "Your bond is true. The first trial is complete."

Elara rose, pulling Gareth to his feet. "Thank you. What's next?"

The lead Guardian approached, their eyes gleaming with approval. "The next trial will test your resilience and your trust in each other. Follow us."

As they moved deeper into the grove, Elara felt a renewed sense of purpose. With Gareth by her side and the guidance of the Guardians, she knew they were ready for whatever lay ahead.

The Guardians led them to a towering ancient tree, its branches reaching up to the heavens. At its base was a doorway, carved with intricate runes that glowed faintly in the dim light. The lead Guardian turned to Elara and Gareth, their expression solemn.

"This is the Tree of Trials," the Guardian said. "Inside, you will face challenges designed to test your resilience and trust. You must rely on each other and the bond you share to succeed."

Elara took a deep breath, feeling Gareth's reassuring presence beside her. "We're ready."

They stepped through the doorway, entering a dark corridor that seemed to stretch infinitely. The air was thick with anticipation, and their footsteps echoed in the silence.

Suddenly, the corridor shifted, and they found themselves in a vast, open space filled with shifting shadows. The darkness seemed to pulse with a life of its own, closing in around them.

"Elara," Gareth said, his voice steady. "We have to stay together. No matter what happens, remember our bond."

Elara nodded, her heart racing. "I won't let go."

The shadows surged forward, forming menacing shapes that circled around them. Elara felt a wave of fear, but she drew strength from Gareth's presence.

"Remember the heartstone," Gareth reminded her. "Use its power to light our way."

Elara focused, feeling the heartstone's energy within her. She raised her hand, and a beam of light shot forth, piercing the darkness. The shadows recoiled, but more kept coming, relentless and unyielding.

"We need to move," Gareth said, his voice urgent. "There's a path through the shadows. We have to find it."

They moved forward, the light from the heartstone guiding their way. The shadows pressed in, testing their resolve, but they held fast, their trust in each other unwavering.

"Elara," Gareth called out as a particularly menacing shadow lunged at them. "Focus on the light. We can do this."

Elara concentrated, pouring her energy into the heartstone. The light intensified, creating a protective barrier around them. The shadows hissed and retreated, unable to penetrate the barrier.

"We're almost there," Gareth said, his voice filled with determination. "Keep going."

As they pressed on, the path ahead became clearer. They could see the end of the corridor, a doorway bathed in light. With a final burst of energy, they broke through the last of the shadows and stepped into the light.

The corridor vanished, and they found themselves back in the clearing, the Guardians waiting for them. The lead Guardian smiled, their eyes filled with pride.

"You have shown great resilience and trust," the Guardian said. "The second trial is complete."

Elara and Gareth stood together, their bond stronger than ever. "Thank you," Elara said, her voice filled with gratitude. "We couldn't have done it without each other."

The Guardians nodded. "You are ready for the final trial. But remember, your greatest strength lies in your bond. Trust in it, and you will succeed."

As they prepared for the final trial, Elara and Gareth knew that whatever challenges lay ahead, they would face them together. Their journey had only just begun, but with the support of the Guardians and their unwavering bond, they were ready to confront the darkness and emerge victorious.

Chapter 8
The Final Trial

The Guardians led Elara and Gareth to a secluded glade, its entrance marked by ancient stones inscribed with runes that glowed faintly in the twilight. The air was thick with the scent of blooming flowers and the hum of unseen magic. In the center of the glade stood an intricately carved stone pedestal, upon which rested an ancient tome.

"This is the Tome of Wisdom," the lead Guardian explained, their voice echoing softly in the stillness. "The final trial will test your wisdom and your ability to make decisions that benefit not just yourselves, but all those you protect."

Elara and Gareth exchanged a determined glance. They stepped forward, approaching the pedestal with a mixture of reverence and anticipation.

"The answers you seek lie within these pages," the Guardian continued. "But be warned: the questions will challenge your beliefs and your resolve. Are you prepared to face them?"

Elara took a deep breath, her fingers brushing the tome's ancient cover. "We are ready."

Gareth nodded, his hand resting reassuringly on Elara's shoulder. "We'll face this together, as we always have."

With a nod from the Guardian, Elara opened the tome. The pages were filled with dense, flowing script, and as she read, the words seemed to come alive, forming images and scenes that played out before them.

The first question appeared, written in glowing script: "What is the most important quality of a leader?"

Elara and Gareth looked at each other, pondering the question. "Compassion," Elara said after a moment. "A leader must care for their people, must understand their struggles and strive to protect them."

Gareth nodded in agreement. "And wisdom. A leader must make difficult decisions and guide their people through dark times with a clear mind."

The tome seemed to absorb their answers, the pages glowing brighter. The next question formed: "What sacrifice are you willing to make for the greater good?"

Elara's heart clenched at the question, her mind racing. "We've already sacrificed so much," she murmured. "But I would give up my powers if it meant saving our village, protecting our people."

Gareth squeezed her hand. "And I would give my life for the same. We must be willing to put others before ourselves, no matter the cost."

The tome's pages turned, revealing the final question: "What binds you together and makes you stronger?"

Elara and Gareth smiled at each other, their answer clear. "Our bond," Elara said confidently. "The trust and love we share. It's what gives us strength and hope."

Gareth nodded. "Our unity is our greatest weapon against the darkness."

The tome glowed brightly, the answers they had given resonating with the magic within. The Guardians stepped forward, their expressions filled with approval and respect.

"You have shown wisdom, compassion, and a willingness to sacrifice for the greater good," the lead Guardian said. "You have passed the final trial."

Elara closed the tome, feeling a sense of completion and resolve. "Thank you for guiding us."

The Guardians nodded. "Your journey is far from over, but you are now equipped with the knowledge and strength you need to face the Shadow King. Remember, your bond is your greatest strength."

Elara and Gareth bowed to the Guardians, their hearts filled with gratitude and determination. As they left the glade, they knew they were ready for whatever lay ahead.

The journey back to the village was filled with a sense of purpose and anticipation. The forest seemed less daunting now, the path clearer and the air lighter. Elara and Gareth walked side by side, their bond stronger than ever after the trials they had faced.

"Elara," Gareth said, breaking the comfortable silence. "I've been thinking about what the Guardians said. About our bond being our greatest strength."

Elara looked at him, her eyes filled with warmth. "What about it?"

Gareth smiled, a hint of vulnerability in his eyes. "I just want you to know that no matter what happens, I'm grateful for you. For us. Facing these challenges together has shown me just how strong we are."

Elara squeezed his hand. "I feel the same way, Gareth. We've been through so much, and I know we can face anything as long as we're together."

As they neared the village, the familiar sounds of life and activity reached their ears. The villagers were hard at work, fortifying defenses and preparing for the Shadow King's inevitable return. Elara and Gareth exchanged a determined glance, knowing their journey was far from over.

They were greeted with cheers and relieved smiles as they entered the village square. Elder Brynn approached them, his eyes filled with pride and curiosity. "Welcome back. What have you learned?"

Elara took a deep breath, ready to share their experiences. "The Guardians have given us guidance and strength. We've faced trials that tested our bond and our resolve. We're ready for the Shadow King."

The villagers gathered around, listening intently as Elara and Gareth recounted their journey. They spoke of the trials, the wisdom they had gained, and the unity that had grown between them.

"We must prepare for the final battle," Gareth said, his voice steady and confident. "The Shadow King will come, and we need to be ready to stand against him."

Thomas, the elder villager, stepped forward. "We're with you. Whatever it takes, we'll fight to protect our home."

Elara nodded, her heart swelling with gratitude and determination. "We can do this. Together, we're stronger than any darkness."

As the villagers dispersed to continue their preparations, Elara and Gareth found a moment of quiet. They stood together, looking out over the village that had become their home and the people who had become their family.

"We've come so far," Elara said softly, her eyes shining with hope.

Gareth wrapped an arm around her shoulders, his voice filled with conviction. "And we'll go even further. This is just the beginning. Together, we'll face whatever comes next."

As the sun set over the village, casting a golden glow over the fortified walls and determined faces, Elara and Gareth knew that their greatest challenges still lay ahead. But they faced the future with a united front, ready to protect their home and each other against the encroaching darkness.

With the wisdom of the Guardians fresh in their minds, Elara and Gareth convened with Elder Brynn and the village council in the makeshift war room. The room was filled with maps, notes, and magical artifacts, all tools they would use to formulate their strategy against the Shadow King.

"We must strike first," Gareth began, pointing to a map that outlined the village and the surrounding forest. "If we wait for him to come to us, we risk losing too much."

Thomas, ever the voice of caution, frowned. "But where do we strike? His forces are vast and his location unknown."

Elder Brynn interjected, his eyes gleaming with ancient knowledge. "The Shadow King draws his power from the Nexus of Shadows, a hidden sanctuary deep within the forest. If we can find and disrupt the Nexus, we weaken him."

Elara nodded, her heart racing with the possibilities. "Then that's where we go. We use the knowledge we've gained and the strength of our bond to find the Nexus and destroy it."

Lila, who had been listening intently, spoke up. "And what about the villagers? We can't leave them undefended."

"We won't," Gareth assured her. "We'll leave a contingent here, led by Thomas. They'll defend the village and ensure its safety while we take the fight to the Shadow King."

The room fell silent as everyone absorbed the plan. The stakes were high, but the path was clear. Finally, Thomas nodded. "It's risky, but it's our best chance. We'll prepare the defenses here and hold the line."

Elder Brynn placed a reassuring hand on Elara's shoulder. "You and Gareth are the key to this. Trust in each other, and trust in the strength you've built together. The Guardians have shown you the way; now you must walk it."

Gareth squeezed Elara's hand, his eyes filled with determination. "We'll return with victory, or not at all."

Elara took a deep breath, her resolve hardening. "Let's prepare. We leave at first light."

As the council disbanded, Elara and Gareth stepped outside, the cool night air a welcome relief. They walked together through the village, the stars shining brightly above them.

"Gareth, do you ever wonder if we're doing the right thing?" Elara asked quietly, her voice filled with uncertainty.

Gareth stopped, turning to face her. "Every day. But I know that as long as we're together, we can face anything. The village, our friends—they're counting on us. And I believe in us."

Elara smiled, feeling the weight of his words. "You always know what to say."

He chuckled softly. "Not always. But I do know that I love you, Elara. And that's enough for me."

Elara felt tears prick at her eyes, but they were tears of gratitude and love. "I love you too, Gareth. And together, we're unstoppable."

As they stood there, bathed in the soft glow of the moonlight, they knew that the battle ahead would be their greatest challenge yet. But they also knew that with each other, they had the strength to face it.

The dawn broke with a promise of a fierce battle. Elara and Gareth, along with a small group of the village's best fighters, set out into the forest. The path to the Nexus was fraught with danger, but they moved with purpose, guided by the Guardians' wisdom and their unyielding resolve.

The forest grew darker as they ventured deeper, the air thick with an oppressive energy. Elara felt the heartstone pulse at her chest, its warmth a comforting presence. "We're getting close," she whispered to Gareth.

He nodded, his eyes scanning the surroundings. "Stay alert, everyone. The Shadow King will have defenses in place."

As if on cue, dark figures emerged from the shadows, their eyes glowing with malevolent intent. The village fighters readied their weapons, but Elara raised a hand. "Let us handle this."

Gareth and Elara stepped forward, their combined power radiating in a visible aura. The shadow creatures hesitated, sensing the strength of their bond. "Now!" Gareth shouted, and together, they unleashed a burst of light that scattered the creatures, dissolving them into nothingness.

The path ahead cleared, they pressed on, the trees thinning until they reached a vast, open space dominated by a towering, dark structure. The Nexus of Shadows. It pulsed with a dark energy, and Elara could feel the malevolence emanating from it.

"This is it," she said, her voice steady. "We need to destroy it."

As they approached, the ground trembled, and the Shadow King appeared, his form towering and cloaked in darkness. "Fools!" he roared. "You think you can defeat me here, in my domain?"

Gareth stepped forward, his sword gleaming. "We don't think. We know."

The battle erupted with a fury. The Shadow King's power was immense, but Elara and Gareth fought with a strength born of their bond and the knowledge they had gained. They moved as one, their attacks synchronized and precise.

"Together, Elara!" Gareth shouted as they launched a combined attack, their energies merging into a powerful beam of light that struck the Shadow King, forcing him to stagger.

"You will not defeat me!" the Shadow King roared, summoning more shadow creatures to his aid.

Elara's eyes blazed with determination. "We will. For our village, for our people!"

She focused the heartstone's power, channeling it through her and into Gareth. Their combined force created a protective barrier that shielded them from the Shadow King's attacks. The air crackled with energy as they pressed forward, their goal clear.

Gareth nodded to Elara, signaling the final move. "Now, Elara. Together."

With a cry of determination, they directed their combined power at the Nexus. The dark structure began to crack, the malevolent energy within it destabilizing. The Shadow King howled in fury and desperation, his form flickering.

"No!" he screamed. "This cannot be!"

But it was too late. The Nexus shattered in a brilliant explosion of light, the dark energy dissipating into the air. The Shadow King's form disintegrated, his power broken.

As the dust settled, Elara and Gareth stood amidst the ruins of the Nexus, their hands still joined, their hearts beating as one. The village fighters, awe-struck and relieved, gathered around them.

"We did it," Elara whispered, her voice filled with exhaustion and triumph. "We really did it."

Gareth smiled, his eyes reflecting the soft glow of the heartstone. "Together."

The journey back to the village was filled with a sense of accomplishment and relief. They had faced the darkness and emerged victorious, their bond stronger than ever. The villagers greeted them with cheers and tears of joy, their faces alight with hope.

Elder Brynn approached, his eyes filled with pride. "You have done what many thought impossible. The Shadow King is defeated, and the Nexus destroyed. The village is safe."

Elara and Gareth stood hand in hand, their hearts swelling with gratitude and love. They had faced their greatest challenge and emerged stronger for it. The future, once shrouded in darkness, now gleamed with the promise of hope and unity.

As the sun set over the village, casting a golden glow over the victorious and the hopeful, Elara and Gareth knew that their journey was far from over. But with their bond, their love, and their unwavering resolve, they were ready to face whatever came next. Together.

Chapter 9
New Beginnings

The village was alive with activity. The echoes of their victory against the Shadow King reverberated through every street and home. While the threat had been vanquished, the scars it left behind were deep, and the process of healing and rebuilding had only just begun. Elara and Gareth, though celebrated as heroes, knew that their work was far from over.

Elara stood in the village square, directing efforts to rebuild the damaged structures. She wore a simple dress, her hands dirty from helping with the construction. It was a stark contrast to the fierce warrior who had stood against the Shadow King. Yet, in this role, she felt equally powerful, knowing she was helping to restore her home.

"Elara, we need more timber for the east wall," Thomas called out, his voice carrying over the clatter of hammers and saws.

Elara nodded, wiping sweat from her brow. "Lila, can you organize a group to fetch more timber from the forest?"

Lila, ever reliable, nodded and quickly gathered a group of villagers. "We'll get it done, Elara. Don't worry."

As they set off, Gareth approached, his presence a comforting anchor amidst the chaos. "How are you holding up?" he asked, his voice filled with concern.

Elara managed a tired smile. "I'm alright. It's just... there's so much to do."

Gareth placed a reassuring hand on her shoulder. "You're doing great. We all are. And remember, you're not alone in this."

Elara looked into his eyes, finding strength in his unwavering support. "Thank you, Gareth. For everything."

He nodded, his gaze sweeping over the bustling village. "We should take a moment to talk to Elder Brynn. He mentioned something about the heartstone and its future."

Elara's curiosity piqued, she agreed. "Alright. Let's find him."

They made their way to Elder Brynn's hut, where the wise elder was sifting through ancient texts. He looked up as they entered, a warm smile spreading across his face.

"Elder Brynn, you wanted to speak with us?" Gareth began.

Brynn nodded, closing the book he was reading. "Yes. The heartstone is a powerful artifact, and now that the immediate threat is gone, we must decide its fate."

Elara glanced at the heartstone, which hung around her neck, its glow a constant reminder of the battle they had fought. "What do you mean?"

Brynn's eyes were thoughtful. "The heartstone's power is immense, but it must be safeguarded. We cannot allow it to fall into the wrong hands. You and Gareth have shown great wisdom and strength. I believe it is up to you to decide how best to protect it."

Elara felt the weight of his words. "We will do whatever it takes to ensure its safety."

Gareth nodded in agreement. "We'll discuss it and come up with a plan."

Brynn smiled, his trust in them evident. "I know you will. Now, go. There is much work to be done, and your people need you."

As they left the hut, Elara felt a renewed sense of purpose. The battle might have been won, but their journey was far from over. Together, she and Gareth would ensure the safety of their village and the heartstone, forging a new future from the ashes of their past.

The sun hung low in the sky, casting long shadows across the village as evening approached. Elara and Gareth gathered the council and key villagers in the meeting hall to discuss the future of the heartstone and the continued defense of their home.

Elder Brynn sat at the head of the table, his presence a calming influence. "Thank you all for coming. We are here to discuss how we can protect the heartstone and ensure the safety of our village."

Thomas spoke up first, his voice practical. "We've fortified the village walls, but we need to ensure that the heartstone is hidden and protected. It's too powerful to be left out in the open."

Lila nodded in agreement. "We should consider placing it in a secret location, known only to a few trusted individuals."

Elara glanced at Gareth, who gave her a reassuring nod. "We've thought about this. The heartstone's power can be both a blessing and a curse. We need a place where it can be safe but also accessible if we need it."

Gareth added, "There's a cave system beneath the village. It's hidden and secure. We could create a chamber within it to house the heartstone."

Elder Brynn nodded thoughtfully. "A wise choice. It will be hidden from prying eyes but still within reach should its power be needed again."

Thomas leaned forward, his brow furrowed. "But who will guard it? We can't just leave it unprotected."

Gareth met his gaze. "We propose creating a small, dedicated group of guardians. They will be trained to protect the heartstone and keep its location secret. Elara and I will oversee their training."

Lila smiled. "I volunteer. I've seen what the heartstone can do, and I want to ensure it remains safe."

Several other villagers echoed her sentiment, volunteering to join the guardians. Elara felt a surge of gratitude and pride. "Thank you all. Together, we'll protect our home and the heartstone."

Elder Brynn raised his hand for silence. "We also need to consider our alliances. The Guardians of the Sacred Grove have been invaluable. We should maintain contact with them and seek out other allies who share our goals."

Gareth nodded. "Agreed. We'll send emissaries to the surrounding villages and realms. We're stronger together."

Elara glanced around the room, seeing the determination in each face. "We've come through so much. This is just the beginning. We'll build a future where our children can grow up in peace."

Thomas smiled, a rare expression for the usually stern elder. "We believe in you, Elara. You've shown us what true leadership looks like."

The meeting continued, plans taking shape and roles being assigned. As the evening deepened, Elara and Gareth stepped outside, the cool night air a welcome relief.

Gareth wrapped an arm around her shoulders. "We're doing the right thing. The village is stronger than ever."

Elara leaned into him, feeling the warmth of his embrace. "Yes, and with you by my side, I know we can face anything."

They stood there in silence, the stars twinkling above, each one a symbol of hope and endless possibilities. The path ahead would be challenging, but together, they were ready to walk it, hand in hand, with the heartstone's light guiding their way.

As they gazed out over their village, now bustling with the energy of rebuilding and renewal, they knew that the future held endless possibilities. And with each step forward, they were creating a legacy of hope, strength, and unity that would endure for generations to come.

In the days that followed the council meeting, the village was a hive of activity. Everyone had a role to play, from fortifying defenses to training the new guardians of the heartstone. Amidst the bustling energy, Elara and Gareth found a rare moment of quiet to reflect on their journey and the road ahead.

They walked together through the forest, the canopy above filtering the sunlight into a mosaic of gold and green. The tranquility of the woods provided a stark contrast to the recent turmoil they had faced. Elara's fingers intertwined with Gareth's, their steps synchronized as they moved through the underbrush.

Elara broke the silence, her voice soft. "It feels like a lifetime ago that we were just trying to survive each day. Now, we're planning for a future."

Gareth nodded, his gaze fixed on the path ahead. "It's amazing how much has changed. And it's because of you, Elara. Your strength and determination have brought us to this point."

Elara blushed, a smile playing on her lips. "I couldn't have done it without you, Gareth. You've been my rock, my partner in all of this."

Gareth stopped walking and turned to face her, his expression serious but filled with love. "We'll continue to face whatever comes our way, together. The Shadow King may be gone, but there will always be challenges. As long as we stand united, we can overcome anything."

Elara felt a surge of emotion, the weight of their bond and their shared journey washing over her. "I believe that too. Together, we are unstoppable."

They continued their walk, the forest's serene beauty providing a backdrop to their quiet contemplation. The challenges they had faced had only strengthened their bond, and the future, though uncertain, felt filled with endless possibilities.

The cave system beneath the village was a hidden marvel, its entrance concealed by thick undergrowth and ancient trees. Elara and Gareth led the newly formed group of guardians into the depths, their torches casting flickering shadows on the walls. The air was cool and damp, the silence only broken by the soft echoes of their footsteps.

Elder Brynn accompanied them, his knowledge of the ancient runes and protective spells crucial to their mission. They reached a large cavern, its natural beauty enhanced by the shimmering crystals embedded in the walls. It was here that they would create the heartstone's sanctuary.

Brynn raised his hands, chanting softly as he inscribed runes around the cavern's perimeter. The runes glowed faintly, forming a protective barrier that would shield the heartstone from any who sought to misuse its power.

"This place is perfect," Brynn said, his voice reverberating in the cavern. "The runes will protect the heartstone, and only those with pure intentions will be able to enter."

Elara approached the center of the cavern, holding the heartstone. Its glow illuminated her face, casting a serene light. "This will be its new home," she said softly, placing the heartstone on a stone pedestal.

Gareth stood beside her, his hand resting on her shoulder. "We've done everything we can to ensure its safety. Now, we must trust in the guardians and each other."

The guardians gathered around, their faces reflecting a mix of reverence and determination. Lila stepped forward, her voice filled with resolve. "We will protect it with our lives. The heartstone is our future, and we will ensure it remains safe."

Brynn nodded, his eyes filled with pride. "You are all entrusted with a great responsibility. Remember the lessons we've learned and the strength of our unity. Together, we can face any challenge."

As they made their way back to the village, Elara and Gareth felt a deep sense of satisfaction. The heartstone was secure, and their village was stronger than ever. But their journey was far from over. They had built the foundations of a new future, and now it was time to nurture and protect it.

Back in the village, the preparations continued. The training of the guardians intensified, with Elara and Gareth leading the exercises. The villagers worked tirelessly, their determination unwavering. The sense of community and shared purpose was palpable, a testament to the strength they had found in each other.

One evening, as the sun set over the horizon, casting a golden glow over the village, Elara and Gareth stood together on the hill overlooking their home. The sight filled them with hope and a sense of accomplishment.

"We've come so far," Elara said, her voice filled with emotion. "And there's still so much to do. But for the first time, I feel truly hopeful about the future."

Gareth nodded, his eyes reflecting the same hope. "We've built something incredible here. A community, a family. And with the heartstone protected, we can focus on building a future filled with peace and prosperity."

Elara turned to face him, her eyes shining. "Whatever challenges come our way, I know we can face them together."

Gareth smiled, taking her hands in his. "Together, always."

As night fell and the stars began to twinkle in the sky, the village below buzzed with activity and life. Elara and Gareth stood as the guardians of this new beginning, ready to lead their people into a future filled with hope, strength, and unity. The heartstone's light, now safely hidden yet ever-present, symbolized the enduring bond and the resilient spirit of their community. They were ready to face whatever came next, hand in hand, with the confidence that they could overcome any darkness together.

Chapter 10
The Dawn of a New Era

The village had transformed remarkably over the past few weeks. The scars left by the Shadow King were slowly healing, replaced by new buildings, fortified defenses, and a renewed sense of community. Elara and Gareth had become symbols of hope and resilience, their leadership guiding the village towards a brighter future.

The village square was abuzz with activity as preparations were underway for a celebration. It was a day to honor their victories, acknowledge their losses, and look forward to the future with optimism. Elara and Gareth moved through the crowd, their presence eliciting smiles and words of gratitude from the villagers.

Elder Brynn stood at the center of the square, his voice carrying over the crowd. "Today, we celebrate not only our survival but our unity and strength. We have faced darkness and emerged victorious. Let us honor those who fought bravely and those we have lost."

Elara stepped forward, her voice filled with emotion. "This celebration is for all of us. Each one of you has played a crucial role in our victory. We have shown that by standing together, we can overcome any challenge."

Gareth nodded in agreement. "We've come a long way, but there's still work to be done. Together, we will continue to build a future where our children can grow up in peace."

The villagers cheered, their faces alight with hope and determination. Lila approached Elara, her eyes shining with pride. "You and Gareth have inspired us all. This celebration is as much for you as it is for us."

Elara smiled, feeling a deep sense of gratitude. "We're all in this together, Lila. This village is our home, and we'll do everything we can to protect it."

As the festivities began, Elara and Gareth took a moment to step aside, watching the joy and laughter that filled the square. "It's moments like these that make everything we've been through worth it," Gareth said softly.

Elara nodded, her heart full. "Yes, it does. And I know we can face whatever comes next, as long as we're together."

The celebration continued into the evening, the village aglow with lanterns and the sounds of music and laughter. Yet, amidst the revelry, Elara and Gareth couldn't shake the feeling that their challenges were far from over. As the night deepened, a sense of unease began to settle over them.

Elder Brynn approached them, his expression grave. "I fear we may not be as safe as we hoped. There are whispers of unrest in the surrounding realms. The defeat of the Shadow King has left a power vacuum, and others may seek to fill it."

Elara felt a chill run down her spine. "What can we do to prepare?"

Brynn sighed, his eyes reflecting the weight of his years. "We must strengthen our alliances and remain vigilant. The heartstone must be protected at all costs. We cannot allow it to fall into the wrong hands."

Gareth nodded, his jaw set with determination. "We'll send emissaries to the neighboring villages and realms. We need to build a coalition to ensure our continued safety."

Elara placed a hand on Gareth's arm, drawing strength from his resolve. "We'll also need to continue training our guardians and fortifying our defenses. We can't let our guard down."

As they discussed their plans, a messenger arrived, breathless and wide-eyed. "There's trouble in the western village. They're being attacked by bandits. They've requested our help."

Elara and Gareth exchanged a look, their decision made in an instant. "We'll go," Elara said firmly. "Gather a team of our best fighters and prepare to leave immediately."

Lila, overhearing the conversation, stepped forward. "I'll lead the team here to protect the village. You can count on us."

Elara nodded, grateful for her friend's unwavering support. "Thank you, Lila. Keep everyone safe."

As the preparations for their departure began, Elara and Gareth took a moment to address the villagers. "We're going to help our neighbors," Gareth announced. "But we leave the village in capable hands. Stay strong and vigilant."

Elara added, "We'll return soon. In the meantime, continue building and protecting our home. We're all in this together."

The villagers nodded, their faces filled with determination. As Elara and Gareth led their team into the night, the celebration continued, a testament to the resilience and unity of their community. They rode swiftly towards the western village, the sounds of the festival fading into the distance.

As they traveled, Gareth spoke, his voice steady. "We'll face this challenge like we've faced all the others. Together."

Elara nodded, her heart filled with resolve. "Yes, together. And we'll show them that we are stronger than ever."

They arrived at the western village as dawn began to break, the first rays of light casting long shadows over the scene of chaos. The village was under siege, flames licking at the wooden structures, and the sounds of battle filling the air.

Gareth drew his sword, his eyes fierce with determination. "Let's show them what we're made of."

Elara felt the heartstone pulse at her chest, its power surging through her. "For our village, for our people," she said, raising her hand to unleash a burst of light.

They charged into the fray, their presence a beacon of hope amidst the chaos. The battle was fierce, but Elara and Gareth fought with the strength and unity that had carried them through so many challenges before. The villagers of the western village, inspired by their bravery, rallied and joined the fight.

As the sun rose higher, the tide of the battle turned in their favor. The bandits, seeing their defeat was imminent, began to retreat. Elara and Gareth, standing side by side, watched as the last of the invaders fled.

"We did it," Elara said, breathless but triumphant.

Gareth nodded, his eyes scanning the horizon. "Yes, but this is just the beginning. We must remain vigilant. The challenges ahead will test us, but I know we can face them together."

Elara took his hand, their bond a source of unwavering strength. "Together, always."

As the villagers of the western village began to rebuild, Elara and Gareth offered their support and guidance. They knew that their journey was far from over, but with each challenge, they grew stronger and more united.

The dawn of a new era had begun, one filled with hope, resilience, and the promise of a brighter future. And as they looked towards the horizon, Elara and Gareth knew that together, they could overcome any darkness and build a legacy of strength and unity that would endure for generations to come.

After the battle at the western village, Elara and Gareth stayed to help with the recovery efforts. The villagers were deeply grateful for their assistance, and as the days passed, a sense of camaraderie and mutual respect grew between the two communities.

One evening, Elara and Gareth sat by a campfire with the village leaders, discussing future plans and alliances. The air was filled with the scent of wood smoke and the sound of crackling flames, creating a warm and intimate atmosphere.

The western village's leader, Maren, leaned forward, her expression earnest. "We owe you our lives. If it hadn't been for your timely intervention, I shudder to think what would have happened."

Gareth shook his head, his voice firm but kind. "We're all in this together. Protecting each other is the only way we'll survive and thrive."

Maren nodded, her eyes reflecting the flickering firelight. "We've been isolated for too long, focusing only on our own survival. It's time we start building stronger connections with our neighbors."

Elara smiled, her heart swelling with hope. "Unity is our greatest strength. By forming alliances, sharing resources, and standing together, we can create a network of support that the Shadow King's remnants or any other threats can't easily break."

A young man from the western village, Tomas, spoke up, his voice filled with determination. "What can we do to help? How can we contribute to this alliance?"

Elara glanced at Gareth, who nodded in encouragement. She turned back to Tomas, her voice thoughtful. "We need to establish regular communication between our villages. We can set up a system of messengers and scouts to share information quickly. And we can organize joint training exercises for our fighters."

Gareth added, "We also need to start thinking about long-term sustainability. Sharing agricultural techniques, trading goods, and pooling resources will make all our villages stronger and more resilient."

Maren's eyes lit up with enthusiasm. "We have fertile land here. We can provide surplus crops in exchange for other goods or services."

Elara nodded, feeling a surge of optimism. "Exactly. And we can send craftsmen to help rebuild and fortify your defenses. Together, we can create a network of villages that support and protect each other."

The discussion continued late into the night, with ideas and plans flowing freely. The sense of solidarity was palpable, and Elara felt a deep sense of fulfillment. They were building something new, something strong and enduring.

As the meeting drew to a close, Maren raised her cup in a toast. "To unity, to strength, and to a brighter future for all our people."

Elara and Gareth joined in the toast, their hearts filled with hope and determination. They knew that the road ahead would not be easy, but they were ready to face it together, with their allies by their side.

The journey back to their own village was filled with a sense of accomplishment and anticipation. Elara and Gareth led their team through the forest, the path now familiar and comforting. The sun was setting, casting a golden glow over the landscape, and the air was filled with the sounds of nature.

As they approached the village, they were greeted with cheers and smiles. The villagers had been anxiously awaiting their return, and the sight of their leaders safe and sound filled them with relief and joy.

Thomas and Lila met them at the village gates, their expressions a mix of pride and concern. "Welcome back," Thomas said, his voice gruff with emotion. "We were worried."

Gareth clasped his shoulder. "Thank you, Thomas. We've secured a strong alliance with the western village. Together, we'll be much stronger."

Lila hugged Elara, her eyes shining. "You've done so much for us. Thank you."

Elara smiled, feeling the warmth of her friend's embrace. "It's all of us, Lila. We're building this future together."

As they entered the village, the sense of community and unity was stronger than ever. The villagers gathered around, eager to hear about the journey and the plans for the future. Elara and Gareth shared their experiences, the hopes they had for the alliance, and the strategies they had discussed.

Elder Brynn stood quietly at the edge of the crowd, his eyes filled with pride. As Elara and Gareth approached, he nodded approvingly. "You have done well. The bonds you have forged will serve us all in the days to come."

Elara took a deep breath, looking out over the faces of her people. "We've come so far, and there's still a long way to go. But with unity and determination, we can face any challenge. Together, we will create a future filled with hope and strength."

Gareth took her hand, their fingers intertwining. "Together," he echoed, his voice filled with conviction.

As night fell and the stars began to twinkle in the sky, the village buzzed with a renewed sense of purpose. They were not just survivors; they were builders of a new era, a community united by a shared vision of peace and prosperity.

Elara and Gareth stood at the heart of this new beginning, ready to lead their people into a brighter future. With the heartstone's light guiding them and the strength of their bond, they knew they could overcome any darkness and create a legacy of hope and unity for generations to come.

Chapter 11
Trials and Tribulations

The village was bustling with its usual morning activities when a lone rider appeared on the horizon, galloping towards the gates with an urgency that immediately caught everyone's attention. Elara and Gareth, in the midst of organizing the day's work, exchanged a glance and hurried to meet the rider.

The rider, a young woman with dirt-streaked cheeks and wild eyes, pulled her horse to a stop just inside the gates. She looked around frantically before her gaze settled on Elara and Gareth. "Please, help," she gasped, almost falling off her horse.

Gareth stepped forward, steadying her. "Take a moment. Catch your breath. What happened?"

The woman took a few deep breaths, her voice trembling. "My name is Anara. My village, to the north... We're under attack. Raiders, they came out of nowhere. We tried to fight, but we're outnumbered. They've taken many captive. We need help."

Elara felt a surge of urgency. "How far is your village?"

"Half a day's ride," Anara replied, desperation clear in her eyes. "Please, we don't have much time."

Gareth turned to the gathered villagers, his voice commanding. "We need a team, our best fighters. We leave immediately."

Thomas, ever ready, stepped forward. "I'll gather the men. We'll be ready to leave within the hour."

Lila approached, concern etched on her face. "Elara, Gareth, be careful. We don't know what we're walking into."

Elara nodded, determination hardening her features. "We'll be ready. Anara, you'll lead us back to your village. Rest for a moment, and then we ride."

As preparations were made, Elder Brynn approached, his expression serious. "Elara, Gareth, this could be a trap. Be vigilant."

Gareth nodded. "We will. But we can't turn our backs on those in need."

Elara looked into Brynn's eyes, her voice steady. "We'll be cautious. We'll come back, I promise."

Anara, having recovered some of her strength, looked at Elara with gratitude. "Thank you. I didn't know if anyone would help us."

Elara placed a reassuring hand on her shoulder. "We help each other. That's how we survive."

As the team gathered and mounted their horses, the weight of the mission settled over them. They rode out, the dust of their departure lingering in the air.

The journey was swift, the urgency of their mission driving them forward. Anara rode alongside Elara and Gareth, her fear palpable but her resolve unshaken. "My family," she whispered, tears glistening in her eyes. "They took my family."

"We'll get them back," Gareth said firmly. "Stay strong."

Elara felt a surge of determination. "Tell us about the raiders. What did they look like? How many were there?"

"Dozens," Anara replied, her voice trembling. "They wore dark cloaks, their faces hidden. They moved with precision, like they had done this many times before. They're led by a man with a scar across his face. He's ruthless."

Gareth exchanged a look with Elara. "We've dealt with worse. We'll figure out their weaknesses."

As they rode, the terrain became more rugged, the path more treacherous. Anara guided them with confidence, despite her fear. "We're close now. Just over that ridge."

They crested the ridge and looked down at the village below, smoke rising from several buildings. The sight filled Elara with a renewed sense of urgency. "We need to move quickly. Gareth, we need a plan."

Gareth surveyed the scene, his mind working rapidly. "We'll split into two groups. One will create a distraction, drawing the raiders away from the main area. The other will move in to rescue the captives."

Thomas, ready as always, nodded. "I'll lead the distraction team. We'll make enough noise to draw their attention."

Elara looked at her team, their faces determined. "Stay focused. We move fast and strike hard. Let's bring these people home."

With their plan in place, they moved down the ridge, the element of surprise on their side. The air was thick with tension, but Elara felt a surge of confidence. They had faced the Shadow King and won. They could handle this.

As they moved into position, Gareth turned to Elara, his voice low but steady. "Ready?"

Elara nodded, her eyes fierce with determination. "Let's do this."

Thomas and his team moved swiftly, their approach masked by the terrain and the sounds of the village. They positioned themselves near a cluster of buildings, waiting for Gareth's signal. The air was tense, every moment charged with anticipation.

Gareth looked at Elara, their connection a source of strength. "On my mark," he whispered, his eyes scanning the village below. "Thomas will create the distraction, and we move in. Remember, our priority is the captives. We get them out safely."

Elara nodded, her heart pounding with a mix of fear and determination. "I'm ready."

Gareth raised his hand, giving the signal. Thomas and his team sprang into action, creating a loud commotion by toppling carts and shouting. The raiders, caught off guard, turned their attention towards the noise.

"Now," Gareth hissed, and they moved swiftly towards the central area where the captives were held.

Anara led them to a makeshift pen, her eyes wide with recognition. "There they are," she whispered, pointing to a group of huddled figures.

Elara's heart ached at the sight. "We need to move fast. Gareth, cover me."

Gareth nodded, his sword ready. "Go."

Elara and Anara moved towards the pen, the sounds of the distraction filling the air. Elara reached the captives, working quickly to break the lock. "We're here to help," she whispered to the frightened villagers. "Stay quiet and follow us."

The lock broke with a satisfying click, and the captives began to move, their eyes filled with a mix of hope and fear. Anara found her family, embracing them tightly. "We're getting out of here," she whispered fiercely.

As they began to move towards safety, a shout rang out. "Intruders!" The raiders had spotted them.

Gareth stepped forward, his sword gleaming. "Elara, go! I'll hold them off."

Elara's heart clenched, but she knew what needed to be done. "Be careful," she whispered, leading the captives towards the ridge.

The raiders rushed towards them, but Gareth stood firm, his movements precise and deadly. "Keep moving!" he shouted, his voice cutting through the chaos.

Elara and the captives moved as quickly as they could, the sounds of battle ringing in their ears. She glanced back, her heart pounding as she saw Gareth fighting valiantly. "Almost there," she urged the captives. "Keep going."

As they reached the ridge, Thomas and his team rejoined them, their distraction successful. "We need to move, now!" Thomas shouted.

They hurried over the ridge, the safety of the forest in sight. Elara's heart raced, her thoughts consumed by Gareth. She turned to Thomas, her voice urgent. "Gareth is still fighting. We need to go back for him."

Thomas nodded, his eyes grim. "We will. Let's get these people to safety first."

They moved swiftly through the forest, the captives' breaths ragged with fear and relief. Once they were a safe distance away, Elara turned to Thomas. "I'm going back."

Thomas grabbed her arm, his grip firm. "We go together."

They moved back towards the village, their hearts heavy with worry. As they approached, the sounds of battle grew louder. Elara's heart leapt as she saw Gareth, still fighting, his movements tireless.

"Gareth!" she shouted, rushing towards him.

Gareth turned, his eyes lighting up with relief. "Elara, get back!"

Elara joined the fight, her power surging as she fought beside Gareth. Together, they pushed the raiders back, their combined strength overwhelming the attackers. The raiders, realizing they were outmatched, began to flee.

As the last of the raiders disappeared into the forest, Elara turned to Gareth, her heart pounding with relief. "Are you okay?"

Gareth nodded, his breath heavy. "I'm fine. Thanks to you."

They stood there, the village around them quiet once more. The danger had passed, but the weight of their mission remained. Elara took Gareth's hand, her voice filled with determination. "We did it. But there's still more to do."

Gareth squeezed her hand, his eyes filled with resolve. "Together, we can face anything."

As they made their way back to the forest, the captives safe and the village secure, Elara felt a renewed sense of purpose. The challenges ahead were many, but with Gareth by her side and the strength of their community, she knew they could overcome any obstacle. Together, they would build a future filled with hope and unity, one step at a time.

The village was eerily quiet, the only sounds the distant cries of the wounded and the crackling of smoldering buildings. Elara and Gareth, their faces set with determination, made their way through the remnants of the once-thriving village. The air was thick with the scent of smoke and blood. Their steps were deliberate, each one bringing them closer to the heart of the conflict. Anara, her face pale but resolute, led the way, her eyes scanning every shadow, every movement with a hawk's vigilance.

"We need to find them," Elara said, her voice low but firm, the urgency of the situation pressing on her. "They could be anywhere."

Gareth nodded, his eyes scanning the horizon. "We'll split up. Anara, you take the western side. We'll cover the eastern."

Anara gave a curt nod, her grip on her sword tightening. "I'll find them. I won't let them get away."

As they moved, the sounds of the battle seemed to echo in Elara's mind, each step reminding her of the lives at stake. She turned to Gareth, her voice barely a whisper over the din. "Gareth, be careful. We don't know how many there are."

Gareth gave her a reassuring smile, though the tension in his eyes was palpable. "We'll be fine, Elara. We've faced worse."

Their path was littered with debris, the remnants of homes and lives disrupted by the raid. The villagers' cries for help and the clanging of metal filled the air. As they reached the outskirts of the village, they saw them—men cloaked in dark attire, their faces obscured by shadows, dragging a group of villagers towards the forest's edge.

"There!" Elara pointed, her voice sharp with urgency. "They've got the captives. We need to move now."

Gareth didn't hesitate. He sprinted forward, his sword raised high, the glint of its blade catching the dying light. "For the village!" he shouted, his voice echoing through the clearing.

The raiders, caught off guard by the sudden attack, hesitated for a moment before retaliating. Elara and Gareth fought side by side, their movements a blur of steel and determination. Elara's blade sliced through the air, meeting its targets with precision. Gareth, with his strength and skill, was a whirlwind of motion, his every strike a testament to his resolve.

"You won't take them!" Elara shouted, her voice filled with fury and resolve. "We won't let you!"

One of the raiders, a towering figure with a scar across his face, lunged at Gareth. Their swords clashed with a resounding clang, the force of their struggle sending sparks flying into the air. Gareth gritted his teeth, pushing back against the raider's relentless assault. "You'll regret coming here!" he growled, his voice low and menacing.

Elara, seeing Gareth's struggle, moved to his side, her sword meeting the raider's with a force that sent him reeling. "Gareth, are you okay?" she asked, her voice filled with concern.

Gareth nodded, wiping the sweat from his brow. "I'm fine. Let's finish this."

As they fought, the villagers, emboldened by their defenders, began to fight back. Anara, having reached the western edge, joined them, her sword flashing through the air with lethal precision. "We're not going anywhere!" she shouted, her voice a battle cry that fueled the villagers' resolve.

With a final, coordinated strike, Elara and Gareth managed to push the raiders back, their enemies retreating into the shadows of the forest. The battle, though hard-fought, was over. The village, though scarred, was safe once more. The villagers, now free, gathered around Elara, Gareth, and Anara, their faces a mix of relief and gratitude.

"Thank you," one villager, an elderly woman with tear-streaked cheeks, whispered, her voice trembling with emotion. "Thank you for saving us."

Elara knelt beside her, her voice gentle. "We're here to protect you. You're safe now."

Gareth stood, his breath heavy, his eyes scanning the faces of the villagers. "We'll rebuild," he said, his voice firm. "We'll make sure this never happens again."

As the villagers began to tend to their wounded and salvage what they could, Elara turned to Gareth, her eyes filled with a fierce resolve. "We need to find out who they are, why they attacked. This can't be the end."

Gareth nodded, his expression grim. "Agreed. We need to know who's behind this, and we need to stop them."

Anara, her face determined, stepped forward. "I know someone. Someone who might know who the raiders are. It's a long shot, but we have to try."

Elara and Gareth exchanged a look, their resolve hardening. "Then we'll go," Elara said, her voice steady. "We'll find them, and we'll make sure they pay for what they've done."

As the sun set over the village, casting long shadows across the land, Elara, Gareth, and Anara prepared to leave. The journey ahead was uncertain, filled with danger and unknowns, but they knew one thing for certain: they would face whatever came next, together.

The forest was silent as they made their way to the edge of the village, the night air crisp and cold. The only sound was the crunch of their boots on the fallen leaves and twigs, the darkness swallowing them whole. Elara walked ahead, her pace steady, her mind racing with thoughts of the battles fought and the ones yet to come. Gareth and Anara followed, their expressions equally serious, each step bringing them closer to the unknown.

"Anara, who is this person you mentioned?" Elara asked, her voice cutting through the silence.

Anara hesitated for a moment before speaking, her voice low. "His name is Kalen. He's a trader who's been in the area for years. He has connections, knows people who move in the shadows. He might have information on the raiders."

Gareth glanced at Elara, his brow furrowed. "A trader? How do we know we can trust him?"

Anara shrugged, a wry smile playing on her lips. "Trust is a luxury we don't have. But Kalen's been around for a long time. He's not one to betray his contacts, especially not to people he's had dealings with for years."

Elara nodded, her expression resolute. "Then we'll find him. We need answers, and we need them now."

As they walked, the darkness around them seemed to close in, the weight of their mission pressing down on them. The village, now just a distant memory, was behind them, the flames and smoke a stark reminder of the danger that still loomed. The path ahead was fraught with uncertainty, but their resolve was unbroken.

They reached the outskirts of the village just as dawn began to break, the first light of day casting a pale glow over the landscape. Anara led them to a small clearing, a hidden path that wound its way deeper into the forest. "This is the way to Kalen's hideout. It's not far from here."

Gareth looked around, his senses on high alert. "Stay sharp. We don't know what's waiting for us."

Anara nodded, her grip tightening on her sword. "We'll be fine. Kalen's not one to make enemies unless he has to."

As they moved through the forest, the sounds of the morning wildlife slowly returned, the distant call of a bird breaking the silence. The path was narrow, the trees close together, their branches forming a natural canopy overhead. Elara led the way, her eyes scanning the shadows for any sign of danger. Gareth and Anara followed, their steps careful, their senses heightened.

After what felt like an eternity, they reached a small clearing, a hut hidden amongst the trees. The smoke from its chimney curled lazily into the morning air, a sign of life in the midst of the wilderness. Elara approached the hut, her hand on the hilt of her sword, her gaze fixed on the door.

"Stay behind me," she said to Gareth and Anara, her voice low but firm.

They nodded, their expressions serious as they waited for Elara to knock on the door. The sound echoed through the clearing, the silence that followed almost deafening. After a moment, the door creaked open, revealing a figure silhouetted by the light from inside. Kalen stepped out, his face weathered and stern, his eyes sharp and calculating.

"Well, if it isn't Elara and Gareth," Kalen said, his voice gravelly with age. "What brings you to my doorstep at this hour?"

Elara stepped forward, her voice steady. "We need information, Kalen. We need to know who's behind the attack on the village."

Kalen's eyes flickered with recognition, his expression hardening. "You're not the only ones looking for answers. The raiders, they're not just a random group. They're part of something bigger, something darker."

Gareth stepped forward, his voice low and urgent. "We don't have much time. Tell us what you know."

Kalen sighed, his gaze shifting between them. "There's a man, a shadow in the night. He goes by many names, but the one you need to know is Valen. He's the leader of the raiders, a ruthless warlord with

Chapter 12
Shadows of the Past

The morning light filtered through the trees as Elara, Gareth, and Anara stood before Kalen's hut. The air was cool and filled with the scents of the forest. Kalen, his face a mask of wariness and wisdom, ushered them inside. The interior of the hut was modest, filled with maps, scrolls, and artifacts collected over years of trading and dealing.

Kalen gestured to a table, motioning for them to sit. "I see you're all eager for answers. But first, tell me what happened. I need to understand the full scope."

Elara exchanged a glance with Gareth before speaking. "Our village was attacked by raiders. They took captives, destroyed homes. We managed to drive them off, but it was clear they were organized. Anara led us here, hoping you could provide information."

Kalen nodded, his eyes thoughtful. "The raiders have been growing bolder. They're not just a random band of thieves. They're part of something much larger, and much more dangerous."

Gareth leaned forward, his expression intense. "You mentioned a man named Valen. Who is he? Why is he targeting us?"

Kalen sighed, running a hand through his graying hair. "Valen is a warlord, ruthless and cunning. He's been gathering forces, consolidating power. He seeks to control the region through fear and dominance. Your village, with its growing strength and unity, poses a threat to his plans."

Anara, her face pale but determined, spoke up. "But why now? Why attack us now?"

Kalen's eyes hardened. "Because he's nearly ready to make his move. He's been waiting, building his army in the shadows. The attack on your village was just the beginning. He's testing your defenses, trying to weaken you before launching a full-scale assault."

Elara felt a chill run down her spine. "What can we do? How do we stop him?"

Kalen looked at each of them in turn, his expression grave. "You must unite with other villages, form a coalition to stand against him. Alone, you don't stand a chance. Together, you might be able to withstand his onslaught. But it won't be easy. Valen's influence runs deep, and his spies are everywhere."

Gareth nodded, his jaw set with determination. "We'll do whatever it takes. We can't let him destroy everything we've built."

Elara's mind raced with possibilities and plans. "Kalen, will you help us? Your knowledge and connections could make all the difference."

Kalen's eyes softened slightly. "I will. But know this: the road ahead will be fraught with danger. You must be prepared for anything."

As they discussed the details, Kalen provided maps and information about Valen's known movements and strongholds. The gravity of their mission settled over them, but so did a sense of resolve. They had faced darkness before and emerged victorious. They would do so again.

Returning to their village, Elara and Gareth wasted no time in rallying the council and key villagers. The news of Valen's impending threat spread quickly, and the air was thick with tension and determination. In the meeting hall, the atmosphere was charged with urgency as they gathered to discuss their next steps.

Elder Brynn stood at the head of the table, his expression solemn. "We have faced great challenges before, but this threat is unlike any other. We must unite with our neighbors to stand a chance against Valen."

Thomas, ever pragmatic, spoke up. "We need to send emissaries to the surrounding villages immediately. We must form alliances and coordinate our defenses."

Lila, her eyes fierce with resolve, added, "We should also fortify our village further. Strengthen our walls, increase our patrols. We can't be caught off guard again."

Elara nodded, her mind racing with strategies. "We'll need to train more fighters, both men and women. Everyone must be prepared to defend our home."

Gareth stood beside her, his voice steady and strong. "And we'll need scouts to keep watch on Valen's movements. We need to know where he is and what he's planning at all times."

Anara, who had been quietly listening, stepped forward. "I'll go to the northern villages. They've been wary of outsiders, but they'll listen to me."

Elara placed a hand on Anara's shoulder, her voice filled with gratitude. "Thank you, Anara. Your courage is an inspiration to us all."

Elder Brynn nodded in agreement. "We must also seek out the Guardians of the Sacred Grove. Their wisdom and power could be crucial in the battles to come."

Thomas, always thinking ahead, added, "We'll need supplies as well. Food, weapons, medicine. We must prepare for a long conflict."

As plans were made and tasks assigned, the villagers dispersed, each person carrying the weight of their responsibilities. Elara and Gareth, however, lingered, discussing the broader strategy.

"We need to make sure our people are not just prepared, but motivated," Gareth said. "Fear can be paralyzing. We need to inspire them."

Elara nodded. "We've shown them our strength before. We need to remind them that we're fighting for our future, for our children's future."

Gareth's eyes met hers, filled with determination and love. "We'll get through this, Elara. Together, we'll lead them to victory."

In the days that followed, the village became a hive of activity. Emissaries were sent out to neighboring villages, carrying messages of unity and urgent pleas for alliance. The training grounds were filled with villagers learning to fight, their determination fueled by the stakes of the battle ahead.

Elara and Gareth worked tirelessly, overseeing the preparations, rallying the spirits of their people. Each day brought new challenges, but also new signs of hope and resilience. The bonds within the village grew stronger, the sense of community deepening as everyone pulled together for a common cause.

One evening, as the sun set and the sky turned a deep shade of violet, Elara and Gareth stood at the edge of the village, looking out over the preparations. The sounds of training and building filled the air, a testament to their people's resolve.

"We're ready," Gareth said quietly, his arm around Elara's shoulders. "Whatever comes, we'll face it together."

Elara nodded, her heart filled with a mixture of pride and anticipation. "Together, we are unstoppable."

As the stars began to twinkle in the night sky, the village below buzzed with life and determination. They were not just preparing for war; they were building a future, one that would be defined by their strength, unity, and unbreakable spirit. And as Elara and Gareth stood there, side by side, they knew that no matter what challenges lay ahead, they would face them with courage and resolve, guided by the light of the heartstone and the strength of their bond.

Days turned into weeks as the village prepared for the impending conflict. The air was thick with anticipation and resolve. Emissaries had been dispatched to surrounding villages, seeking alliances and support. The training grounds were filled with the clanging of swords and the determined grunts of villagers honing their skills. Elara and Gareth worked tirelessly, their leadership inspiring all who watched.

One morning, as the first light of dawn crept over the horizon, the sound of hooves echoed through the village gates. The emissaries were returning. Elara and Gareth hurried to meet them, their hearts pounding with anticipation.

Thomas, leading the group, dismounted and approached them, his face grim yet resolute. "We've secured alliances with three neighboring villages. They'll send fighters and supplies, but they're wary. Valen's reach is long, and his threats have them on edge."

Elara nodded, absorbing the news. "That's a good start. Did they offer any intelligence on Valen's movements?"

Thomas exchanged a glance with Anara, who stepped forward. "The northern villages reported increased raider activity. They believe Valen is consolidating his forces in the mountains. They've seen movements that suggest he's preparing for a major assault."

Gareth's eyes narrowed with determination. "We need to fortify our defenses even further and prepare for his attack. We can't afford to be caught off guard."

Elder Brynn, who had joined them, listened intently. "And the Guardians of the Sacred Grove? Did they respond?"

Anara shook her head, her expression troubled. "No word from them yet. We sent the message, but they're elusive. We can't count on their help."

Elara felt a pang of disappointment but quickly masked it with resolve. "We'll make do with what we have. Our alliances are crucial. We must stand united."

Thomas stepped closer, his voice low but filled with conviction. "The other villages have agreed to a meeting here, in our village. They want to discuss strategies and solidify our plans."

Gareth nodded. "Good. We'll host them and show them our strength. Together, we can face Valen and his forces."

As they dispersed to continue their preparations, Elara and Gareth stood together, their minds racing with the weight of their responsibilities.

"We've made progress," Gareth said quietly, his hand resting on Elara's shoulder. "But there's still so much to do."

Elara looked into his eyes, finding strength in his unwavering resolve. "We'll get through this, Gareth. Together, we'll lead our people to victory."

The village buzzed with renewed energy as news of the alliances spread. Everyone worked with a sense of purpose, knowing that their efforts were part of a larger plan. The sound of construction and training filled the air, a testament to their collective determination.

As the sun set, casting a golden glow over the village, Elara and Gareth found a moment of quiet reflection. They stood on a hill overlooking the bustling activity below, their hearts filled with a mix of hope and anticipation.

"We're ready," Elara said softly, her gaze fixed on the horizon. "Whatever comes, we'll face it together."

Gareth squeezed her hand, his voice filled with conviction. "Together, we are unstoppable."

The day of the council meeting arrived, and the village was a hive of activity. Leaders from the allied villages gathered in the meeting hall, their faces reflecting the gravity of the situation. The atmosphere was tense but filled with a shared determination.

Elder Brynn called the meeting to order, his voice carrying over the murmurs of conversation. "We are here today to forge a united front against Valen. We must pool our resources, share our intelligence, and stand together if we are to have any hope of defeating him."

Maren, the leader of the western village, spoke first. "Our scouts have confirmed increased activity in the mountains. Valen is gathering his forces, preparing for a major assault. We need to strike first, catch him off guard."

Thomas nodded in agreement. "We've fortified our defenses and trained new fighters, but we need a coordinated attack. We must hit him where he's vulnerable."

Anara, representing the northern villages, added, "We can provide additional fighters and supplies. But we need a clear plan. Valen is ruthless and cunning. We can't underestimate him."

Elara and Gareth exchanged a glance before stepping forward. Elara spoke first, her voice steady and filled with determination. "We've gathered as much intelligence as we can. Valen's stronghold is in the mountains, but he has outposts scattered throughout the region. We need to disrupt his supply lines and weaken his forces before launching a direct assault."

Gareth continued, his tone confident. "Our village will be the staging ground. We'll coordinate the attacks and provide support. But we need everyone's commitment. This is a fight for our survival."

The leaders murmured in agreement, their resolve strengthening. Maren stood again. "We're with you. Together, we can bring Valen down."

Elder Brynn nodded, his eyes reflecting the collective determination of those gathered. "Then it's settled. We move forward with our plans. May our unity be our strength."

As the meeting adjourned, the leaders dispersed to relay the plans to their respective villages. Elara and Gareth remained behind, discussing the finer details with Elder Brynn and the other key leaders.

"We'll need to coordinate our movements carefully," Brynn said. "Communication will be crucial."

Elara nodded. "We've established a network of messengers. They'll keep us informed of any developments."

Gareth added, "We'll also need to ensure the safety of our villagers. The non-combatants must be protected. We can't afford to leave them vulnerable."

Elder Brynn placed a hand on Elara's shoulder. "You've done well, both of you. Your leadership has brought us to this point. Now we must see it through."

As they left the meeting hall, the weight of the coming conflict settled over them. The road ahead would be fraught with danger, but they faced it with a united front and unwavering resolve.

Elara and Gareth walked through the village, the sounds of preparation filling the air. The villagers worked tirelessly, their faces reflecting a mix of fear and determination. Elara felt a surge of pride for her people, their strength and resilience inspiring her.

"We're ready," Gareth said quietly, his gaze fixed on the horizon. "For whatever comes, we'll face it together."

Elara nodded, her heart filled with resolve. "Together, we are unstoppable."

As the sun set, casting a golden glow over the village, Elara and Gareth stood side by side, their hearts filled with hope and determination. They knew that the coming days would test their strength and resolve, but they were ready to face whatever challenges lay ahead, united by their bond and their unwavering commitment to their people.

Chapter 13
The Gathering Storm

The village was a hive of activity as the final preparations for the assault on Valen's stronghold were made. The allied forces had gathered, their combined strength a testament to the unity and determination of the surrounding villages. Elara and Gareth moved through the bustling camp, their presence a steadying influence on the troops.

Elara stopped to speak with Maren, who was overseeing the distribution of supplies. "How are the preparations coming?" she asked, her voice calm but urgent.

Maren looked up, her face lined with fatigue but resolute. "We're almost ready. The fighters are equipped, and the supplies are being distributed. We'll be ready to move by dawn."

Gareth joined them, his eyes scanning the activity around them. "Good. We need to ensure that everyone knows their roles. Communication will be key once the battle begins."

Thomas approached, his expression serious. "The scouts have reported increased activity near Valen's stronghold. He's reinforcing his defenses. We need to move quickly."

Elara nodded, her mind racing with plans and strategies. "We'll hold a final briefing with the leaders tonight. Everyone needs to be clear on the plan."

Anara, who had been coordinating with the northern villages, joined the group. "The northern fighters are ready. They're eager to prove themselves."

Elara smiled, grateful for the support. "Thank you, Anara. Your leadership has been invaluable."

Anara nodded, her eyes shining with determination. "We're all in this together. We'll do whatever it takes to protect our homes."

As the sun began to set, casting a warm glow over the camp, the leaders gathered in the central tent for the final briefing. Elder Brynn, Maren, Thomas, Anara, and other key figures formed a circle around the map spread out on the table.

Elara began, her voice steady. "Our objective is to weaken Valen's forces and disrupt his plans. We'll split into three groups. Group one will attack the outposts, drawing his forces away from the stronghold. Group two will cut off his supply lines. Group three, led by Gareth and me, will lead the main assault on the stronghold."

Gareth pointed to the map, outlining the positions. "Timing is crucial. We need to coordinate our attacks to maximize the impact. We'll use signal fires to communicate our progress."

Thomas spoke up, his voice filled with confidence. "We've trained for this. Our fighters know what's at stake. We won't let you down."

Maren added, "We need to be prepared for anything. Valen is cunning and ruthless. We must stay alert and adaptable."

Elder Brynn nodded, his eyes filled with wisdom and resolve. "Remember, our strength lies in our unity. Trust in each other and in the bond we share. Together, we can overcome any challenge."

Elara felt a surge of pride and determination. "We move at dawn. Rest well tonight. Tomorrow, we fight for our future."

As the meeting adjourned, Elara and Gareth stepped outside, the night air cool and refreshing. They walked together through the camp, the quiet hum of preparations a comforting backdrop.

Gareth turned to Elara, his eyes reflecting the starlight. "We're ready, Elara. Whatever happens tomorrow, we'll face it together."

Elara nodded, her heart swelling with love and resolve. "Together, always."

Dawn broke with a quiet intensity, the first light of the sun casting long shadows over the camp. The fighters, armored and ready, gathered in their designated groups, their faces set with determination. Elara and Gareth moved among them, offering words of encouragement and final instructions.

Thomas approached Elara, his eyes reflecting a mix of anticipation and resolve. "We're ready, Elara. The scouts are in position, and the signal fires are set. We'll be watching for your signal."

Elara nodded, her voice steady. "Thank you, Thomas. Keep your wits about you. We'll need everyone at their best."

Gareth, standing nearby, addressed the assembled fighters. "This is it. Today, we fight not just for our village, but for all the villages. For our families, our future. Stay strong, stay united, and we will prevail."

The fighters responded with a cheer, their spirits lifted by his words. As they dispersed to their positions, Elara and Gareth shared a moment of quiet determination.

"We're ready," Elara said softly, her eyes meeting Gareth's. "Let's end this."

They led their group towards the forest, the path taking them closer to Valen's stronghold. The tension was palpable, every step bringing them closer to the confrontation that would decide their future.

As they neared the stronghold, the signal fires from the other groups flared to life, indicating the start of the attack. The sounds of battle echoed through the forest, the clash of steel and the cries of fighters filling the air.

Elara raised her hand, signaling their group to advance. "For the village!" she shouted, her voice cutting through the chaos.

The fighters surged forward, meeting Valen's forces head-on. The battle was fierce and chaotic, the ground quickly becoming a maelstrom of movement and sound. Elara and Gareth fought side by side, their movements synchronized, their bond giving them strength.

A raider lunged at Elara, his sword aimed at her heart. She parried his blow, her blade flashing in the sunlight as she countered with a swift strike that sent him sprawling. Gareth, facing his own opponent, fought with a fierce intensity, his sword a blur as he defended and attacked with equal skill.

"Stay close!" Gareth shouted, his eyes never leaving the battle in front of him.

Elara nodded, her focus unwavering. "I'm right here!"

As they pushed forward, the tide of the battle began to turn in their favor. The fighters, inspired by Elara and Gareth's leadership, fought with renewed vigor. The signal fires continued to burn, marking their progress and keeping the groups coordinated.

Elara spotted Valen in the midst of the fray, his presence a dark and ominous shadow. She felt a surge of anger and determination. "Gareth, there he is. We need to take him down."

Gareth followed her gaze, his expression hardening. "Together."

They fought their way towards Valen, cutting through the raiders with a fierce determination. Valen, seeing them approach, raised his sword, a cruel smile playing on his lips.

"So, you've come to die, have you?" Valen sneered, his voice dripping with contempt.

Elara stepped forward, her eyes blazing with defiance. "No. We've come to end this."

The battle between them was intense, the clash of their swords ringing out over the battlefield. Valen fought with a ruthless precision, his attacks relentless. But Elara and Gareth, fueled by their bond and their resolve, matched him blow for blow.

As the battle raged around them, the fighters continued to press forward, their combined strength overwhelming Valen's forces. The signal fires flared brighter, marking their progress and signaling their impending victory.

With a final, coordinated strike, Elara and Gareth managed to disarm Valen, their swords at his throat. "It's over," Elara said, her voice filled with resolve.

Valen glared at them, his eyes filled with hate. "This isn't the end. Others will come."

Gareth tightened his grip on his sword. "We'll be ready for them. But for now, you're finished."

As Valen was taken into custody, the sounds of battle began to fade, replaced by the cheers of victory. The fighters, exhausted but triumphant, gathered around Elara and Gareth, their faces alight with relief and joy.

"We did it," Elara said, her voice trembling with emotion. "We really did it."

Gareth nodded, his eyes filled with pride. "Together, we can face anything."

As the sun set over the battlefield, casting a golden glow over the scene, Elara and Gareth stood side by side, their hearts filled with hope and determination. They had faced the darkness and emerged victorious, their bond stronger than ever. And as they looked out over the fighters and the future they had fought so hard to protect, they knew that together, they could overcome any challenge that lay ahead.

The battle was over, but the village was still buzzing with the energy of victory. Fighters tended to their wounds, others began the somber task of burying the fallen, and leaders from the allied villages gathered to discuss the next steps. Elara and Gareth stood at the center of it all, their presence a beacon of hope and strength.

Elder Brynn approached them, his face a mixture of pride and concern. "You've done well, both of you. But this victory, while significant, is only the beginning. We must ensure our defenses remain strong and our alliances firm."

Gareth nodded, his expression serious. "Agreed. Valen may be defeated, but his followers are still out there. We need to stay vigilant."

Elara looked around at the weary but determined faces of their people. "We'll send out scouts to monitor any movements and gather intelligence. We can't let our guard down."

Thomas, who had been listening, stepped forward. "I'll lead the scouting parties. We need to keep an eye on the surrounding areas and report any suspicious activity."

Anara joined them, her eyes filled with resolve. "We also need to strengthen our ties with the other villages. They've seen our strength and unity. Now is the time to solidify those bonds."

Maren, leader of the western village, nodded in agreement. "We've seen what we can achieve together. Let's formalize our alliance and ensure we stand as one against any future threats."

Elder Brynn's eyes gleamed with approval. "A council of the allied villages would be wise. A united front will deter any who might seek to take advantage of this time of rebuilding."

Elara turned to Gareth, her hand slipping into his. "We'll convene the leaders and set a date for the first council meeting. This is our chance to create a lasting peace."

Gareth squeezed her hand, his voice filled with confidence. "We've faced the darkness and come through stronger. We'll build a future that honors those we've lost and protects those we love."

As the leaders dispersed to carry out their tasks, Elara and Gareth took a moment to walk through the village, their steps slow and thoughtful. The sky was painted with the colors of twilight, and the air was filled with a sense of quiet determination.

"Do you think we're ready for what comes next?" Elara asked, her voice soft but steady.

Gareth looked at her, his eyes filled with unwavering faith. "With you by my side, Elara, I believe we can face anything. We've proven that together, we are unstoppable."

Elara smiled, her heart swelling with love and pride. "Then let's make sure we're ready. For our village, for our future."

The next few weeks were a blur of activity as the village and its allies worked tirelessly to rebuild and strengthen their defenses. The first council meeting of the allied villages was set to take place, and preparations were underway to host the event. The village buzzed with a mixture of anticipation and hope.

On the day of the council, the meeting hall was filled with representatives from the surrounding villages. The air was thick with the weight of their shared history and the promise of a united future. Elara and Gareth stood at the head of the table, their presence commanding and reassuring.

Elder Brynn called the meeting to order. "We gather here today not just as allies, but as friends and protectors of our homes. Our victory over Valen has shown us the power of unity. Now, we must solidify our bonds and plan for the future."

Maren spoke first, her voice clear and confident. "The western village stands with you. Together, we can create a network of support that will deter any future threats."

Thomas added, "We've seen the strength of our combined forces. Let's establish regular communication and joint training exercises to keep our skills sharp and our defenses strong."

Anara, representing the northern villages, nodded in agreement. "We'll share our resources and knowledge. The northern villages are committed to this alliance and to the safety of all our people."

Gareth turned to Elara, his voice filled with pride. "Elara and I have discussed the need for a council of leaders to oversee our collective efforts. This council will ensure that we remain united and prepared for any challenges that come our way."

Elara continued, her voice steady and inspiring. "We've proven that together, we are stronger. Let's formalize this alliance and create a future where our children can grow up in peace and prosperity."

The representatives voiced their agreement, the room filled with a sense of unity and resolve. The council was officially established, and plans were made for regular meetings and joint initiatives.

As the meeting concluded, the leaders mingled, discussing strategies and sharing stories of their villages. The atmosphere was one of camaraderie and mutual respect, a stark contrast to the tension and uncertainty that had once pervaded their interactions.

Elara and Gareth stepped outside, the cool evening air a welcome relief. They walked to the edge of the village, where the lights of the campfires flickered in the twilight.

"We've done it," Elara said, her voice filled with a mixture of relief and pride. "We've built something truly remarkable."

Gareth nodded, his eyes reflecting the glow of the fires. "And we'll keep building. Together, we'll create a future that honors our past and protects our people."

Elara leaned into him, her heart swelling with love and gratitude. "Together, always."

As they stood there, the village around them alive with the sounds of celebration and hope, they knew that their journey was far from over. But with each other and their unwavering commitment to their people, they were ready to face whatever challenges lay ahead. Together, they would build a legacy of strength, unity, and peace that would endure for generations to come.

Chapter 14
A New Dawn

The village had settled into a rhythm of cautious optimism. The new alliances had brought a sense of security, and the shared efforts in rebuilding and fortification had strengthened the bonds between the allied villages. Elara and Gareth, however, remained vigilant, knowing that the calm might be temporary.

One morning, as the first light of dawn painted the sky in shades of pink and gold, Elara and Gareth stood on the hill overlooking their village. The sight filled them with a sense of pride and determination. The peaceful scene was a stark contrast to the chaos they had faced not long ago.

"It's beautiful, isn't it?" Elara said softly, her gaze fixed on the village below.

Gareth nodded, his arm around her shoulders. "It is. We've come so far, Elara. But we can't let our guard down. Valen's followers are still out there, and we need to be ready for anything."

Elara sighed, a mixture of relief and lingering anxiety in her voice. "I know. But it's hard not to hope for some lasting peace."

Gareth squeezed her shoulder gently. "Hope is important. It keeps us going. But we need to balance it with preparation."

As they spoke, Anara approached, her expression serious. "Elara, Gareth, we need to talk. There's been a development."

They turned to face her, concern etched on their faces. "What is it, Anara?" Elara asked.

Anara took a deep breath. "Our scouts have reported unusual activity in the eastern forests. It seems like Valen's followers are regrouping. There have been sightings of raiders moving through the area, and they appear to be gathering resources and recruiting fighters."

Gareth frowned. "So they're not done yet. We need to address this before it becomes a larger threat."

Elara nodded, her resolve hardening. "We need to gather the council and plan our next move. We can't let them regain their strength."

They made their way back to the village, their steps brisk with urgency. The council convened in the meeting hall, the atmosphere charged with a mix of determination and tension. Elder Brynn, Maren, Thomas, and the other leaders were already assembled, their faces reflecting the seriousness of the situation.

"Elara, Gareth, what's the news?" Elder Brynn asked, his voice steady.

Anara stepped forward, addressing the council. "Our scouts have confirmed that Valen's followers are regrouping in the eastern forests. They're gathering resources and recruiting fighters. We need to act quickly."

Maren's eyes narrowed. "We can't let them rebuild. If they gain enough strength, they could launch another attack."

Thomas nodded in agreement. "We need a plan. A coordinated effort to disrupt their activities and prevent them from becoming a threat again."

Elara glanced at Gareth, then addressed the council. "We propose a two-pronged approach. We'll send a team to gather more intelligence and confirm their exact location and strength. Simultaneously, we'll prepare our forces for a potential strike."

Gareth added, "We need to be strategic. A direct assault might be too risky without more information. Our scouts will be crucial in this effort."

Elder Brynn nodded thoughtfully. "Agreed. We need to be cautious but decisive. Let's mobilize our scouts and prepare our fighters. We can't afford to wait."

As the council members began to outline their tasks and coordinate their efforts, Elara felt a renewed sense of purpose. The challenges ahead were daunting, but she knew they had the strength and unity to face them.

The next day, the leaders gathered once more to finalize their plans. The meeting hall buzzed with activity as maps were spread out and strategies discussed. The air was thick with anticipation, the weight of their mission clear on everyone's faces.

Thomas stood at the head of the table, addressing the assembled leaders. "Our scouts have returned with detailed reports. The raiders are camped in a heavily wooded area, making a direct assault difficult. We need to approach this carefully."

Elara leaned over the map, her finger tracing the scout's route. "We can use the terrain to our advantage. A small, agile team could infiltrate their camp and gather more intelligence or disrupt their operations."

Maren nodded. "A larger force could remain hidden nearby, ready to strike if needed. We need to hit them hard and fast, minimizing our exposure."

Anara, ever practical, added, "We'll need to ensure communication between our teams. Signal fires or messenger birds could work, but we need to be prepared for any contingencies."

Gareth spoke up, his voice steady. "We'll lead the infiltration team. We're familiar with their tactics, and we can adapt quickly if things go awry."

Elder Brynn's eyes met Elara's, his expression serious. "This mission is dangerous, but it's necessary. We must trust in our unity and our planning."

As the final details were ironed out, the leaders dispersed to prepare their respective teams. Elara and Gareth gathered their fighters, briefing them on the plan and ensuring everyone was ready for the mission ahead.

That evening, as the sun set and the campfires flickered in the twilight, Elara and Gareth took a moment to reflect on the task ahead. They stood at the edge of the camp, the sounds of preparation and quiet conversations filling the air.

"We've faced worse," Elara said, her voice filled with determination. "We can do this."

Gareth nodded, his gaze fixed on the horizon. "Together, we can face anything."

As night fell, the camp settled into a tense but focused quiet. Elara and Gareth joined their team, readying themselves for the mission. The air was filled with the scent of pine and the promise of a challenging but necessary battle ahead.

At dawn, the infiltration team set out, moving quietly through the forest. The path was rugged, the trees thick and shadowed, but their resolve was unshakable. They moved with purpose, their goal clear: to disrupt Valen's followers and prevent them from becoming a threat once more.

As they neared the raider's camp, Elara signaled for the team to halt. She and Gareth moved ahead, their senses heightened, every shadow and sound scrutinized. The camp came into view, a makeshift fortification nestled among the trees, its occupants unaware of the approaching danger.

Gareth whispered, "We need to find a way to weaken their defenses. If we can cause enough chaos, it will give our larger force the advantage they need."

Elara nodded, her mind racing with possibilities. "Let's find their supply stores. If we can destroy those, it will cripple their operations."

They moved stealthily through the camp, avoiding patrols and staying in the shadows. The tension was palpable, but their training and unity kept them focused. As they reached the supply stores, Elara set to work, planting charges and preparing for the attack.

Gareth kept watch, his eyes scanning the camp. "We're almost ready. Just a little longer."

Elara finished her task, signaling to the team. "It's time. Let's get out of here and light the signal."

They retreated silently, the forest providing cover as they moved back to their rendezvous point. Once at a safe distance, Elara lit the signal fire, the flames a beacon of their readiness.

Within moments, the larger force moved in, their attack swift and coordinated. The camp erupted in chaos, the raiders caught off guard and disorganized. Elara and Gareth joined the fray, their presence a rallying point for their fighters.

The battle was fierce but brief, their planning and execution proving decisive. As the last of the raiders fled, Elara and Gareth stood amidst the wreckage, their breaths heavy but victorious.

"We did it," Elara said, her voice filled with relief and triumph.

Gareth nodded, his eyes reflecting the flickering flames. "Together, we are unstoppable."

As the sun rose, casting a golden glow over the forest, the fighters gathered, their faces alight with hope and determination. They had faced the darkness and emerged stronger, their unity and resolve a beacon for the future.

Elara and Gareth knew that there would always be challenges ahead, but with each other and their unwavering commitment to their people, they were ready to face whatever came next. Together, they would build a future of strength, unity, and enduring peace.

The aftermath of the raid on Valen's camp left the village buzzing with a mixture of relief and renewed determination. The successful mission had crippled Valen's followers, but everyone knew the fight was far from over. Elara and Gareth returned to their village, where the council convened to discuss the next steps.

The meeting hall was filled with the hum of conversation as leaders from the allied villages gathered. Elder Brynn called the meeting to order, his voice carrying over the noise. "We've dealt a significant blow to Valen's forces, but we cannot afford to be complacent. We need to assess our position and plan our next move."

Maren spoke first, her tone confident. "Our scouts have confirmed that Valen's forces are scattered and disorganized. Now is the time to strike, to ensure they cannot regroup."

Thomas nodded in agreement. "We should launch a coordinated offensive to root out the remaining raiders. They're vulnerable, and we can't give them time to recover."

Elara leaned forward, her eyes sharp with determination. "We need to be strategic. Our strength lies in our unity and our ability to plan carefully. A reckless attack could cost us dearly."

Gareth added, "We should divide our forces to cover more ground. Small, agile teams can track down the scattered raiders while the main force remains here to defend the village."

Anara, representing the northern villages, voiced her support. "We can provide additional fighters for the search teams. Our knowledge of the terrain will be invaluable."

Elder Brynn considered their words, then nodded. "Very well. We will form three search teams, each supported by fighters from different villages. We must act swiftly and decisively."

The leaders began to outline their plans, assigning roles and responsibilities. The air was charged with a sense of purpose and resolve.

Elara turned to Gareth, her voice low but firm. "We'll lead the first team. We know their tactics and can adapt quickly if needed."

Gareth agreed, his expression serious. "We'll take the northern route. Anara, can your fighters join us?"

Anara nodded. "Of course. We'll move out at first light."

Thomas spoke up, addressing the council. "We need to ensure communication between the teams. Signal fires worked well during the raid, but we'll also use messengers to relay information quickly."

Maren added, "We should also prepare the village for a possible counterattack. Valen's followers might try to strike back in desperation."

Elder Brynn's eyes gleamed with approval. "Good. Let's make our final preparations. We move at dawn."

As the meeting adjourned, Elara and Gareth took a moment to discuss their strategy with Anara and the other team leaders. The weight of their responsibility was heavy, but their resolve was unshakable.

"We need to be ready for anything," Elara said, her voice steady. "Stay sharp and communicate constantly. We can't afford any mistakes."

Gareth nodded. "We'll coordinate our movements and make sure we're always one step ahead of the raiders."

Anara smiled, her confidence unwavering. "We've got this. Together, we're unstoppable."

The dawn was cool and crisp as the teams set out, the first light of day casting long shadows over the village. Elara, Gareth, Anara, and their fighters moved through the forest with quiet determination, their senses alert to any signs of the raiders.

Elara signaled for a halt, her eyes scanning the dense underbrush. "We need to stay focused. They could be anywhere."

Gareth moved beside her, his voice low. "We'll find them. We've trained for this."

Anara, leading a group of scouts, returned with news. "We've found tracks leading east. They're trying to move quickly, but they're leaving a trail."

Elara nodded, her eyes sharp. "Let's follow them. Stay close and stay quiet."

The group moved swiftly but cautiously, their movements synchronized and precise. The forest was dense, the sounds of wildlife masking their approach. As they neared a clearing, Elara raised her hand, signaling for silence.

"They're just ahead," she whispered. "We need to surround them and cut off their escape."

Gareth and Anara nodded, moving to position their fighters. The air was thick with tension, every rustle of leaves and snap of a twig magnified in the silence.

With a swift, coordinated movement, they launched their attack. The raiders, caught off guard, scrambled to defend themselves. Elara and Gareth fought side by side, their blades flashing in the morning light.

"Stay together!" Gareth shouted, his voice carrying over the sounds of battle. "Don't let them regroup!"

Elara parried a blow from a raider, her movements fluid and precise. "We've got them on the run. Keep pushing!"

Anara, leading a flanking maneuver, cut through the raiders' defenses, her fighters pressing the advantage. "They're falling back! We've almost got them!"

The raiders, disorganized and demoralized, began to retreat. Elara signaled for a final push, her voice filled with determination. "Don't let them escape! We need to finish this!"

The fighters surged forward, overwhelming the remaining raiders. The clearing was filled with the sounds of clashing steel and shouted commands, but slowly, the battle turned in their favor. The last of the raiders fell or fled, their forces shattered.

Breathing heavily, Elara surveyed the scene, her heart pounding with the adrenaline of victory. "We did it," she said, her voice filled with relief. "They're finished."

Gareth moved beside her, his expression both exhausted and triumphant. "We couldn't have done it without everyone's efforts. This was a true team victory."

Anara joined them, her face flushed with exertion but alight with triumph. "The northern fighters were incredible. We've proven that our alliance is strong."

Elara nodded, her eyes meeting Gareth's. "Together, we can face any challenge. We've shown that today."

As the fighters regrouped, tending to their wounded and securing the area, Elara and Gareth took a moment to reflect on their journey. They had faced immense challenges and had emerged stronger for it.

"We need to head back and report to the council," Gareth said, his voice steady. "They need to know that the threat is over."

Elara agreed. "And we need to ensure that our defenses remain strong. There's always the possibility of new threats."

As they made their way back through the forest, the weight of their victory settled over them. They had faced the darkness and emerged victorious, their bond and unity stronger than ever.

Back at the village, they were greeted with cheers and relief. The council gathered to hear their report, their faces reflecting the mixture of relief and pride that Elara and Gareth felt.

Elder Brynn stood, his eyes filled with gratitude. "You've done a remarkable thing. You've secured our future and shown the power of unity."

Maren, Thomas, and Anara echoed his sentiments, their voices filled with pride and determination.

Elara looked around at the faces of their allies and friends, her heart swelling with hope. "We've proven that together, we are unstoppable. Let's continue to build a future of strength and unity."

Gareth took her hand, his voice filled with conviction. "Together, always."

As they stood before their people, the sun setting behind them, Elara and Gareth knew that they had built something truly remarkable. Their journey was far from over, but with each other and their unwavering commitment to their people, they were ready to face whatever challenges lay ahead. Together, they would build a legacy of strength, unity, and enduring peace.

Chapter 15
The Path to Peace

The village was a hive of activity as people went about their daily tasks, their spirits lifted by the recent victory. Elara and Gareth found a moment of quiet in the midst of the bustle, walking through the gardens they had helped cultivate. The scents of blooming flowers and fresh earth filled the air, a testament to the resilience and renewal of their community.

Elara paused by a bed of lavender, her fingers brushing the fragrant blossoms. "It’s hard to believe how much we’ve been through," she said softly, her voice filled with a mix of wonder and reflection.

Gareth nodded, his gaze fixed on the horizon. "We’ve faced so many challenges, but we’ve always found a way through. Together."

Elara turned to him, her eyes searching his. "Do you ever think about what might have been? If we hadn’t found the heartstone, if we hadn’t fought back?"

Gareth’s expression grew thoughtful. "I do. But then I remember that everything we’ve done has brought us here. We’ve built something beautiful out of the ashes of our struggles."

They continued their walk, the sounds of the village fading into the background. As they approached the edge of the gardens, they saw Elder Brynn sitting on a bench, his eyes closed as he soaked in the morning sun.

"Elder Brynn," Elara called gently, her voice filled with warmth.

Brynn opened his eyes, a smile spreading across his face. "Elara, Gareth. Join me."

They sat beside him, the peace of the moment enveloping them. "It’s good to see the village thriving," Brynn said, his voice tinged with pride. "You’ve both done so much to bring us here."

Elara smiled, her heart swelling with gratitude. "We couldn't have done it without everyone's help. The strength of our community is what makes us resilient."

Brynn nodded. "And what do you see for our future?"

Gareth leaned forward, his eyes filled with determination. "We need to continue building our alliances, ensuring that our defenses are strong and that we're prepared for any new challenges. But more than that, we need to nurture the peace we've fought so hard for."

Brynn's gaze turned thoughtful. "Peace is not just the absence of conflict. It's the presence of justice, of unity, of shared purpose. You've set us on the right path, but there's still much work to be done."

Elara reached out, placing a hand on Brynn's. "We're committed to that work. For our children, and for the future of all our people."

Gareth added, "And we'll do it together. That's the lesson we've learned through all of this. Unity is our greatest strength."

Brynn's eyes shone with pride. "You two are the heart of this village. Your bond is what inspires others to strive for better. Never forget that."

They sat in silence for a moment, the weight of Brynn's words settling over them. The path ahead was clear, but it was also filled with new challenges and opportunities.

As they rose to leave, Brynn spoke again. "Remember, peace is a journey, not a destination. It's something we must work for every day."

Elara and Gareth nodded, their hearts filled with resolve. "We will," Elara said, her voice steady. "Every day."

Later that afternoon, the council gathered in the meeting hall, the atmosphere charged with a sense of purpose and anticipation.

Representatives from the allied villages had joined them, their faces reflecting the hope and determination that had become the hallmark of their alliance.

Elder Brynn stood at the head of the table, his presence commanding yet welcoming. "We've gathered here today to discuss our next steps. Our victory has given us a moment of respite, but we must not become complacent."

Maren spoke first, her voice filled with urgency. "The remnants of Valen's forces are still out there. We need to track them down and ensure they can't regroup."

Thomas nodded in agreement. "We've strengthened our defenses, but we need to go on the offensive. Strike at the heart of any remaining threats before they can strike at us."

Anara, ever practical, added, "We also need to focus on rebuilding. Many of our villages have suffered losses. We need to ensure our people have the resources they need to recover fully."

Elara glanced at Gareth, then addressed the council. "We propose a two-pronged approach. First, we will send out scouting parties to locate any remaining raiders. Once we have their locations, we can plan coordinated strikes to eliminate them. Second, we'll establish a network of resource-sharing among our villages to support each other in the rebuilding efforts."

Gareth continued, his voice steady and confident. "We'll need volunteers for the scouting parties and for the rebuilding teams. This is a collective effort, and every contribution matters."

Maren smiled. "The western village is ready to provide fighters for the scouting parties. We've also begun gathering supplies to share with those in need."

Thomas added, "Our scouts are already trained and prepared. We'll coordinate with the other villages to cover as much ground as possible."

Anara's eyes gleamed with determination. "The northern villages will send both fighters and resources. We're committed to seeing this through."

Elder Brynn nodded approvingly. "Your unity and commitment are what will ensure our success. Let's finalize our plans and begin the preparations immediately."

As the council members dispersed to relay the plans to their respective villages, Elara and Gareth lingered, discussing the details with Elder Brynn.

"We need to ensure that communication remains strong," Gareth said. "Signal fires and messengers worked well, but we should also consider more permanent solutions."

Elara nodded. "We could establish regular meetings of the council, rotating between the villages. It would keep everyone informed and strengthen our bonds."

Brynn's eyes twinkled with approval. "A wise suggestion. Regular communication is crucial to maintaining our unity."

As they left the meeting hall, Elara and Gareth felt a renewed sense of purpose. The challenges ahead were significant, but they had faced greater trials and emerged stronger for it.

Walking through the village, they saw the faces of their people filled with hope and determination. Children played in the streets, their laughter a testament to the peace that had been hard-won. The sounds of construction and the sight of new growth in the gardens were reminders of the resilience and strength of their community.

"We've built something amazing here," Elara said, her voice filled with pride.

Gareth nodded, his eyes shining with love and resolve. "And we'll keep building. Together, we'll create a future that honors our past and protects our people."

As the sun set, casting a warm glow over the village, Elara and Gareth stood hand in hand, ready to face whatever challenges lay ahead. With their unity and unwavering commitment, they knew they could overcome any obstacle and build a legacy of strength, peace, and enduring hope for generations to come.

The next morning, the village awoke to the sounds of bustling activity. The sun had barely risen, but the preparations for the scouting and rebuilding efforts were already underway. Elara and Gareth found a brief moment of respite in the midst of the chaos, standing at the edge of the village where the forest began.

Elara gazed at the trees, her mind filled with thoughts of the journey ahead. "It feels like we've been fighting for so long. I wonder if there will ever be a time when we can truly rest."

Gareth stepped closer, his hand gently touching her shoulder. "We've built a foundation for peace, Elara. It might not be perfect or immediate, but every step we take brings us closer."

She turned to face him, her eyes reflecting a mixture of hope and uncertainty. "Do you ever worry that we're not doing enough? That despite all our efforts, there will always be another threat?"

Gareth's expression softened, and he took her hands in his. "I do. But I also know that what we're doing matters. Every act of kindness, every alliance we form, strengthens the future we're building. We're not just fighting for ourselves, but for those who come after us."

Elara nodded, her resolve returning. "You're right. We can't lose sight of what we're fighting for. We need to keep moving forward, no matter how difficult it gets."

Gareth smiled, his confidence infectious. "Together, we can face anything. And when the time comes to rest, we'll know we've earned it."

The village square was filled with people as the leaders gathered to address the community. The air was charged with a mix of anticipation and determination. Elara and Gareth stood at the forefront, their presence a steadying influence on the crowd.

Elder Brynn raised his hand, calling for silence. "Friends, today marks the beginning of a new chapter in our journey. We've faced many challenges, but we've also achieved great victories. Now, we must continue our work to ensure lasting peace and security for our people."

Maren stepped forward, her voice clear and strong. "Our scouts have identified several areas where Valen's followers might be hiding. We will form teams to search these areas and ensure that no threat remains."

Thomas added, "We also need to focus on rebuilding. The damage to our villages is extensive, and it's essential that we support each other in the recovery process. We'll establish teams to coordinate resources and efforts across the allied villages."

Anara, representing the northern villages, spoke next. "Our commitment to this alliance is unwavering. We'll provide fighters and resources to support both the scouting and rebuilding efforts."

Elara addressed the crowd, her voice filled with determination. "This is a collective effort. Every person here has a role to play, whether it's in the scouting parties, the rebuilding teams, or supporting those efforts in other ways. Our strength lies in our unity."

Gareth continued, "We must remain vigilant and proactive. We've seen what we can achieve together, and we cannot afford to let our guard down. Let's move forward with purpose and resolve."

The crowd responded with cheers and applause, their spirits lifted by the leaders' words. As people began to organize into their respective teams, Elara and Gareth took a moment to speak with Elder Brynn.

"Your leadership has been invaluable," Brynn said, his voice filled with pride. "You've shown us what true strength and unity look like."

Elara smiled, her heart swelling with gratitude. "We've learned from the best, Elder Brynn. Your guidance has been a beacon for us all."

Brynn's eyes twinkled with approval. "Continue to lead with the same wisdom and compassion. The path to peace is long, but it's a journey worth taking."

As the teams prepared to set out, Elara and Gareth joined the first scouting party. The forest was dense and shadowed, the air filled with the sounds of nature. They moved with purpose, their senses alert to any signs of danger.

"Stay close and stay quiet," Elara whispered to the group. "We need to cover as much ground as possible without alerting any potential threats."

Gareth led the way, his eyes scanning the underbrush. "If we find anything, we regroup and plan our next move. No one goes off alone."

The hours passed in a tense but steady search. They found traces of campsites and tracks, evidence that the raiders had been in the area but had moved on. Each discovery was meticulously recorded and relayed back to the village.

As the sun began to set, casting long shadows through the trees, Elara called for a halt. "We've covered a lot of ground today. Let's set up camp and continue in the morning."

The group gathered around a small fire, the warmth and light a welcome respite from the day's efforts. They shared stories and plans, their bond strengthened by the shared mission.

Elara turned to Gareth, her voice filled with quiet determination. "We're making progress. Every step we take brings us closer to ensuring our future is secure."

Gareth nodded, his gaze steady. "We'll keep pushing forward. Together, we can overcome any obstacle."

As the night settled in, Elara and Gareth took a moment to reflect on their journey. They had faced countless challenges, but they had also achieved incredible victories. The road ahead was still fraught with uncertainty, but they knew they were not alone.

"We've come so far," Elara said softly, her eyes meeting Gareth's. "And we'll go even further."

Gareth's hand found hers, their fingers intertwining. "Together, always."

The forest around them was quiet, a serene backdrop to their resolve. They had built something remarkable, and they were ready to continue their journey. With each other and the unwavering support of their community, they knew they could face whatever challenges lay ahead and build a legacy of strength, unity, and enduring peace.

Chapter 16
Trials of Unity

The village awoke to the sound of alarm bells ringing through the crisp morning air. Elara and Gareth, already on high alert, quickly gathered their weapons and hurried to the village square. A scout, breathless and wide-eyed, was speaking urgently with Elder Brynn.

"What's happened?" Elara demanded, her heart pounding.

The scout, a young man named Joren, caught his breath. "We spotted a group of raiders near the western border. They were heavily armed and moving quickly. It looks like they're planning an attack."

Gareth frowned, his jaw set with determination. "How many are there?"

"Too many for a small group," Joren replied. "At least fifty, maybe more."

Elder Brynn turned to Elara and Gareth, his expression grave. "We need to act quickly. We can't let them catch us off guard."

Elara nodded, her mind racing with strategies. "We'll need to split our forces. Some will stay to defend the village, and the rest will move to intercept the raiders before they get too close."

Maren, who had joined them, spoke up. "My fighters are ready. We can take the western flank and set up an ambush."

Thomas added, "We'll fortify the village defenses and prepare for a possible breach."

Elara looked at Gareth, her eyes filled with resolve. "We'll lead the intercepting force. We need to stop them before they reach the village."

Gareth nodded, his grip on his sword tightening. "Let's move quickly. We don't have much time."

As they organized their forces, Elara took a moment to address the gathered fighters. "This is not just about defending our home. It's about protecting our future, our children, and everything we've built together. Stay strong, stay united, and we will prevail."

The fighters responded with a unified cheer, their spirits lifted by her words. As they prepared to move out, Elara and Gareth took one last look at the village, their hearts heavy with the weight of their responsibility.

"Be careful," Elder Brynn said, his voice filled with concern. "May the Guardians watch over you."

Elara and Gareth nodded, their determination unwavering. "We'll return," Elara promised, her voice steady. "With victory."

The intercepting force moved swiftly through the forest, the sounds of their passage muted by the dense underbrush. Elara and Gareth led the way, their senses heightened, every movement and sound scrutinized.

"We need to be ready for anything," Gareth whispered. "They could have scouts of their own."

Elara nodded, her eyes scanning the trees. "We'll take them by surprise. We have to."

As they approached the area where the raiders had been spotted, Maren's group moved into position, setting up an ambush along the narrow path. The tension was palpable, every breath and heartbeat magnified in the silence.

"They're coming," Joren whispered, his voice barely audible.

Elara and Gareth signaled their fighters to hold their positions. The sound of marching feet and clinking armor grew louder, and soon the first raiders came into view, their faces grim and determined.

"Wait for my signal," Elara murmured, her eyes fixed on the approaching enemy.

The raiders moved closer, unaware of the danger lurking in the shadows. When they were almost upon them, Elara raised her hand and gave the signal. The ambush was swift and decisive. Arrows flew from the trees, and fighters surged forward, catching the raiders off guard.

"For the village!" Gareth shouted, his voice a rallying cry.

The battle was fierce, the air filled with the clash of steel and the cries of the wounded. Elara and Gareth fought side by side, their movements fluid and synchronized, their bond giving them strength.

"We've got them on the run!" Maren shouted, her sword flashing in the morning light.

Elara's eyes blazed with determination. "Don't let them regroup! Keep pushing!"

The raiders, disorganized and demoralized, began to retreat. The fighters pressed their advantage, driving the enemy back. As the last of the raiders fled into the forest, a cheer rose from the victorious fighters.

"We did it," Gareth said, his breath heavy but triumphant.

Elara nodded, her eyes scanning the battlefield. "We need to make sure they don't come back. Let's secure the area and then return to the village."

With the immediate threat neutralized, the fighters moved to secure the area, ensuring no raiders remained hidden in the forest. Elara and Gareth coordinated with Maren and Thomas, their leadership ensuring a thorough sweep.

"We need to leave a few scouts here," Maren suggested. "In case they try to regroup or send reinforcements."

Gareth agreed. "Good idea. Joren, pick a few of your best and stay on watch. Report back if you see any movement."

Joren nodded, selecting a small team and positioning them strategically around the area. "We'll keep an eye out."

As they completed their sweep, Elara gathered the fighters to address them. "You've all done an incredible job. This victory is a testament to our unity and strength. But we must remain vigilant. We can't afford to let our guard down."

Thomas added, "Let's return to the village and reinforce our defenses. We need to be prepared for anything."

The journey back to the village was filled with a mix of relief and exhaustion. The fighters, though weary, held their heads high, proud of their accomplishment. As they approached the village, the sight of their home brought a renewed sense of purpose.

Elder Brynn and the villagers greeted them with cheers and gratitude. "You've done it!" Brynn exclaimed, his eyes shining with pride. "You've protected us once again."

Elara dismounted, her legs feeling the strain of the long day. "It was a team effort, Elder Brynn. Everyone played their part."

Gareth joined her, addressing the gathered villagers. "We've secured the area, but we need to stay vigilant. Let's reinforce our defenses and make sure we're ready for any future threats."

The villagers quickly set to work, following Gareth and Elara's instructions. The atmosphere was one of determination and solidarity, the recent victory bolstering their spirits.

As the sun set, casting a warm glow over the village, Elara and Gareth found a moment of quiet by the central fire. The day's events had taken their toll, but their resolve was stronger than ever.

"We did it," Elara said, her voice filled with a mix of relief and pride. "We protected our home."

Gareth smiled, his hand finding hers. “And we’ll keep doing it. Together, we can face anything.”

Elder Brynn joined them, his expression one of quiet satisfaction. “You’ve shown us what true leadership and unity look like. The village is stronger because of you.”

Elara shook her head, her eyes reflecting the firelight. “We’re all in this together, Elder Brynn. This village’s strength comes from everyone who calls it home.”

Gareth nodded, his gaze steady. “We’ll continue to lead and protect. For our future and for the future of those who come after us.”

The night settled in, the village bathed in the soft glow of the fires. The sounds of laughter and conversation filled the air, a testament to the resilience and unity of the community. Elara and Gareth stood hand in hand, their hearts filled with hope and determination.

They had faced another challenge and emerged victorious. The path to lasting peace was long, but with their unwavering commitment and the support of their people, they knew they could build a future of strength, unity, and enduring hope. Together, they were unstoppable.

The next day, the village was alive with renewed energy. The recent victory had bolstered the spirits of the villagers, but Elara and Gareth knew they had to keep the momentum going. They gathered the council and representatives from the allied villages to discuss the next steps.

Elder Brynn, standing at the head of the table, addressed the group. "We have won an important battle, but our journey is far from over. We must strengthen our defenses and continue to build our alliances."

Maren nodded, her expression serious. "The western village is ready to provide additional resources and fighters. We need to ensure that every village is prepared for any future threats."

Thomas added, "We should also establish a permanent communication network between our villages. Regular updates and quick responses are crucial."

Elara spoke up, her voice steady. "We've seen the strength of our unity. Let's formalize this alliance with a treaty. Each village will pledge to support one another in times of need, sharing resources and information."

Anara, representing the northern villages, agreed. "A treaty will solidify our commitment to each other. We can draw up the terms and have representatives from each village sign it."

Gareth leaned forward, his eyes filled with determination. "We should also set up a rotating council, with leaders from different villages taking turns to oversee our collective efforts. This will ensure that every village has a voice."

Elder Brynn's eyes gleamed with approval. "A wise suggestion, Gareth. Let's finalize the details and prepare for a signing ceremony."

As the council members discussed the specifics of the treaty and the communication network, the atmosphere was charged with purpose and resolve. Elara and Gareth's leadership had inspired confidence and a sense of shared destiny among the allied villages.

Once the meeting concluded, Elara and Gareth took a moment to speak with Elder Brynn privately. "We've come a long way, but there's still so much to do," Elara said, her voice filled with both pride and determination.

Brynn nodded, his expression thoughtful. "Your vision and dedication have brought us here. Continue to lead with the same strength and wisdom, and our alliance will thrive."

Gareth placed a hand on Brynn's shoulder. "Thank you, Elder Brynn. Your guidance has been invaluable. We'll make sure this alliance stands the test of time."

As they walked through the village, Elara and Gareth spoke with various villagers, listening to their concerns and ideas. The sense of community and shared purpose was palpable, and the bonds between the people were stronger than ever.

"We need to keep fostering this sense of unity," Elara said, her eyes reflecting the determination she felt. "It's what will see us through any challenges we face."

Gareth nodded, his voice filled with conviction. "Together, we can overcome anything."

The day of the signing ceremony arrived, and the village square was transformed into a space of celebration and solemnity. Banners from each of the allied villages fluttered in the breeze, and a large table was set up in the center, adorned with the symbols of unity and peace.

The villagers gathered, their faces filled with hope and anticipation. Elara and Gareth stood at the forefront, their presence a source of strength and inspiration. Elder Brynn began the ceremony with a few words.

"We gather here today to formalize our alliance, a testament to our shared commitment to peace and mutual support. This treaty represents more than just words on parchment. It symbolizes the strength of our unity and the hope for a brighter future."

Maren, Thomas, Anara, and other representatives from the allied villages stepped forward, each signing the treaty with solemn determination. As Elara added her signature, a wave of emotion washed over her. This was a moment of triumph, a culmination of all their efforts and sacrifices.

Gareth took her hand, his voice low but filled with pride. "We've done it, Elara. This is the beginning of something truly remarkable."

Elara smiled, her eyes shining. "It is. And we'll continue to build on this foundation, for our children and for generations to come."

As the ceremony concluded, the villagers erupted into cheers, their voices filling the air with joy and celebration. Music and laughter echoed through the village as people danced and shared stories, the weight of recent battles momentarily lifted.

Elara and Gareth moved through the crowd, their hearts filled with hope and determination. They spoke with villagers and leaders, reinforcing the bonds that had been forged through shared struggle and triumph.

"We've achieved so much," Elara said softly, looking out over the joyful scene. "But there's still more to do."

Gareth nodded, his gaze steady. "We'll face it together, just as we always have. With unity and resolve, there's nothing we can't accomplish."

As the sun set, casting a warm glow over the village, Elara and Gareth stood hand in hand, ready to embrace the future. The path ahead was filled with challenges, but it was also filled with promise and potential.

With the strength of their community and the unbreakable bonds of their alliance, they knew they could face any obstacle and build a future of peace, prosperity, and enduring hope. Together, they were unstoppable, and their vision for the future shone brightly in the hearts of all who stood with them.

Chapter 17
Rising Challenges

The village thrived in the days following the signing ceremony. The newfound unity among the allied villages was palpable, and efforts to rebuild and fortify continued with renewed vigor. Elara and Gareth, however, remained vigilant, knowing that peace was fragile and must be constantly protected.

One morning, as Elara walked along the forest's edge, checking the perimeter defenses, she noticed something unusual. A rustle in the underbrush, too deliberate to be an animal. Her hand instinctively went to the hilt of her sword.

"Who's there?" she called out, her voice steady but commanding.

A figure emerged from the shadows, hands raised in a gesture of peace. It was a young woman, her clothes tattered and eyes wide with a mix of fear and determination. "Please, I mean no harm. I seek refuge."

Elara's eyes narrowed, but she did not lower her guard. "Who are you? What brings you here?"

The woman stepped closer, her voice trembling. "My name is Seraphina. I escaped from Valen's camp. I have information that could help you."

Elara's grip on her sword relaxed slightly. "Information? Why should we trust you?"

Seraphina's gaze was steady, despite her evident exhaustion. "Because I have nothing left to lose. Valen's forces are planning another attack, but this time they aim to strike at your heart, the leaders of this village."

Elara's heart pounded as she processed the information. "Come with me. You need to speak with Gareth and the council."

As they made their way to the village square, Elara couldn't shake the feeling of impending danger. She found Gareth overseeing the training of new recruits and quickly briefed him on the situation.

"Gareth, this is Seraphina. She claims to have escaped from Valen's camp and has vital information about an upcoming attack."

Gareth's expression hardened as he turned to Seraphina. "Tell us everything."

Seraphina took a deep breath, her voice steadying. "Valen is desperate. He's gathering all the forces he can muster for a final assault. He plans to target the leaders to throw the villages into chaos. He believes that without you, the alliance will crumble."

Gareth exchanged a look with Elara. "We need to alert the council immediately."

They hurried to the meeting hall, where Elder Brynn and the other leaders were already gathering. The atmosphere was tense as Seraphina recounted her tale, detailing Valen's plans and the state of his forces.

Thomas, ever pragmatic, spoke first. "If what she says is true, we need to prepare for an immediate attack. We can't afford to be caught off guard."

Maren nodded in agreement. "We should fortify our defenses and ensure that our communication lines are secure. We need to be ready for anything."

Elder Brynn turned to Seraphina, his eyes filled with a mix of gratitude and suspicion. "You've risked much to bring us this information. Why did you come to us?"

Seraphina's eyes shone with sincerity. "Because I believe in what you're building here. Valen's way is one of destruction and fear. I want to be part of something better."

Elara felt a surge of determination. "We need to trust her. And we need to act fast. Let's strengthen our defenses and prepare for the worst."

Gareth stood, his voice filled with resolve. "We'll double the patrols and set up a perimeter around the village. We won't let Valen catch us unprepared."

The village was a whirlwind of activity as preparations for the impending attack were set in motion. Every able-bodied person had a role to play, whether it was fortifying the defenses, gathering supplies, or training for combat. Elara and Gareth coordinated the efforts, their leadership vital in maintaining order and morale.

Elara approached the training grounds where new recruits were being put through their paces. "Remember, it's not just about strength. It's about strategy and working together. Stay focused and trust in your comrades."

Gareth was nearby, overseeing the construction of additional barricades. He turned to Thomas, who was directing a group of builders. "We need these finished by nightfall. Speed is important, but so is precision. Make sure they're sturdy."

Thomas nodded, his face set with determination. "We'll get it done, Gareth. We've faced worse and come out stronger."

As the sun began to set, casting long shadows across the village, the council gathered for a final briefing. The tension was palpable, but so was the resolve to protect their home and people.

Elder Brynn addressed the group, his voice steady. "We've done all we can to prepare. Now, we must trust in our efforts and each other. Remember, our strength lies in our unity."

Maren added, "Our scouts will keep watch and alert us to any movement. We need to be ready to respond at a moment's notice."

Elara and Gareth stood at the center, their presence a steadying influence. "We'll take shifts to ensure everyone is rested and ready," Elara said. "Communication is key. If you see anything, report it immediately."

Gareth looked around at the gathered leaders and fighters. "We've faced Valen's forces before and won. We can do it again. Stay strong, stay united, and we will prevail."

The group dispersed to their posts, the air filled with a mix of anticipation and determination. Elara and Gareth took a moment to themselves, standing at the edge of the village where the forest began.

"We're ready," Elara said softly, her eyes scanning the darkening horizon. "Whatever comes, we'll face it together."

Gareth nodded, his hand finding hers. "Together. Always."

As night fell, the village settled into a tense but focused quiet. The sounds of the forest and the distant murmur of voices were the only interruptions. Elara and Gareth moved through the village, checking on the defenses and offering words of encouragement to the fighters.

"Stay sharp," Gareth said to a group of archers positioned at the northern edge. "If you see anything unusual, light the signal fire immediately."

Elara stopped by the group preparing the signal fires, ensuring they had everything they needed. "We'll be in the central square. If anything happens, we'll coordinate from there."

The hours passed slowly, each moment filled with the weight of anticipation. As midnight approached, a low whistle cut through the silence. One of the scouts, a young woman named Liora, ran into the square, her face pale.

"They're coming," she panted, her eyes wide with fear and determination. "From the east. A large force, moving quickly."

Elara and Gareth sprang into action, their training and leadership taking over. "Positions!" Elara shouted, her voice carrying through the village. "Everyone to your posts!"

Gareth moved to the central square, where the council members were gathering. "This is it. Remember your training and stay focused. We've prepared for this."

The village erupted into organized chaos as fighters moved to their positions, weapons at the ready. The signal fires were lit, casting an eerie glow over the defenses. The sound of approaching footsteps and clinking armor grew louder, the enemy drawing closer.

Elara and Gareth stood at the forefront, their presence a beacon of strength and resolve. "Hold the line," Gareth commanded, his voice steady. "We will protect our home."

As the first raiders emerged from the shadows, a fierce battle cry rose from the village defenders. The clash of steel and the cries of battle filled the air, the fight for their home and future truly begun. Elara and Gareth fought side by side, their bond and determination driving them forward.

Together, they faced the darkness, their hearts united in the unyielding resolve to protect everything they held dear.

The village was plunged into chaos as Valen's forces descended upon them. The clash of steel, the cries of the wounded, and the commands of the leaders echoed through the night. Elara and Gareth fought at the forefront, their movements a seamless dance of strength and precision.

"Hold the line!" Gareth shouted, his voice cutting through the din. "Push them back!"

Elara parried a blow from a raider, her sword flashing in the torchlight. "We can't let them break through. Keep your formation tight!"

Maren, leading a group of archers, called out from her position. "Archers, ready! Aim for the ones trying to flank us!"

Thomas, wielding a massive hammer, fought beside Gareth. "We need to cut off their reinforcements. They're sending more from the eastern side!"

Gareth nodded, his eyes scanning the battlefield. "Elara, take a team and flank them. We'll hold the front."

Elara signaled to a group of fighters, her voice firm. "Follow me. We're going to cut them off at the pass."

As they moved swiftly through the chaos, Seraphina appeared, her face determined. "I'm coming with you. I know their tactics."

Elara gave her a curt nod. "Stay close. We need every advantage."

They weaved through the fighting, reaching the eastern side where more raiders were pouring in. Elara raised her sword, her voice a rallying cry. "For the village!"

With a coordinated effort, they attacked the incoming raiders, disrupting their formation. Seraphina's knowledge of their tactics proved invaluable, and they managed to push the reinforcements back.

"Keep pushing!" Elara shouted, her eyes blazing with determination. "We're turning the tide!"

Gareth, still holding the front line, saw their progress and felt a surge of hope. "We've got them on the run! Don't let up!"

Elder Brynn, standing with a group of defenders, called out to the villagers. "Remember what we're fighting for! Our home, our future!"

The villagers, inspired by his words and the bravery of their leaders, fought with renewed vigor. The raiders, realizing they were losing ground, began to falter.

Thomas, swinging his hammer with devastating force, grinned at Gareth. "Looks like we're winning!"

Gareth nodded, his expression grim but determined. "We can't get complacent. Stay alert."

As the battle raged on, Elara and her team continued to disrupt the raiders' reinforcements. Seraphina, fighting fiercely beside her, shouted, "They're falling back! We've broken their line!"

Elara's heart pounded with adrenaline. "Press the advantage! Don't let them regroup!"

The raiders, now in disarray, began to retreat. The village defenders, sensing victory, pushed them further back, reclaiming their ground. As the last of the raiders fled into the forest, a triumphant cheer rose from the villagers.

"We did it," Elara said breathlessly, her eyes scanning the battlefield. "We've defended our home."

Gareth approached, his sword still at the ready. "We need to secure the area and tend to the wounded. This isn't over yet."

Maren and Thomas joined them, their faces reflecting a mix of exhaustion and relief. "We've pushed them back, but they'll regroup," Maren said. "We need to be ready for a counterattack."

Elara nodded, her resolve unshaken. "We'll be ready. This victory is just the beginning."

The first light of dawn began to break over the horizon, casting a pale glow on the battlefield. The villagers moved swiftly to secure the area, gathering the wounded and fortifying their defenses. Elara and Gareth coordinated the efforts, their leadership crucial in maintaining order.

Elder Brynn approached them, his face lined with concern. "We've won a significant battle, but we must remain vigilant. Valen's forces are weakened, but they're not defeated."

Elara's eyes hardened with resolve. "We'll stay alert. We can't let our guard down for a moment."

Gareth looked at the villagers working tirelessly to secure their home. "We need to use this time to strengthen our defenses and prepare for any retaliation. This fight is far from over."

Maren, overseeing the fortifications, called out to them. "We've set up additional barricades and positioned more archers. We'll be ready for whatever comes next."

Thomas, helping to tend to the wounded, added, "Our people are strong. We've shown that we can stand against any threat."

As the village settled into a tense but determined calm, Elara and Gareth found a moment of quiet reflection. They stood at the edge of the village, watching the sunrise and thinking about the battles yet to come.

"We've achieved so much," Elara said softly, her eyes on the horizon. "But we have to keep fighting. For our home, and for our future."

Gareth nodded, his hand finding hers. "Together, we can face anything. We've proven that time and again."

Elara smiled, her heart swelling with love and determination. "Together, always."

As the sun rose higher, bathing the village in its warm light, Elara and Gareth knew that their journey was far from over. The challenges ahead would be many, but with their unity and unwavering commitment, they were ready to face whatever came next. They had defended their home once more, and they would continue to fight for the peace and prosperity of their people.

With the strength of their community and the bonds they had forged, Elara and Gareth stood ready to lead their people into a future filled with hope and promise. Together, they were unstoppable, and their vision for a better world shone brightly in their hearts.

Chapter 18
Unveiling Secrets

The village was beginning to settle back into a semblance of normalcy, the immediate threat of Valen's forces having been repelled. Yet, beneath the surface, there was a lingering tension. Elara and Gareth knew that the danger wasn't truly over. They convened a meeting with the council to discuss the next steps.

Elder Brynn started the meeting, his voice carrying a note of urgency. "We've done well to defend our home, but Valen's forces are still out there. We need more information about their movements and their plans."

Thomas leaned forward, his expression serious. "Our scouts have reported that Valen is regrouping, but we need to know more. We need to find his base of operations."

Seraphina, who had integrated herself into the village's efforts, spoke up. "I might be able to help with that. I've seen maps and heard conversations while I was in his camp. I think I can guide us to his stronghold."

Elara's eyes narrowed thoughtfully. "It's a risk, but it might be our best chance to end this threat once and for all. What do you need to find it?"

Seraphina took a deep breath. "A small, fast-moving team. We need to avoid detection and gather as much information as possible. Once we have the location, we can plan a coordinated strike."

Gareth nodded. "I'll lead the team. We'll take only the best scouts and fighters. Speed and stealth will be crucial."

Maren interjected, "I'll prepare our forces here. Once we have the information, we'll be ready to move at a moment's notice."

Elder Brynn looked around the table, his eyes filled with determination. "This mission is critical. The fate of our villages depends on its success. Elara, Gareth, Seraphina—this is your task. Make sure it succeeds."

Elara and Gareth exchanged a glance, their resolve mirrored in each other's eyes. "We won't fail," Elara said, her voice firm.

Later that evening, as they prepared for the mission, Elara and Gareth walked through the village, speaking with those who would stay behind. The villagers' faces reflected a mix of hope and anxiety, but their trust in their leaders was unwavering.

"We're counting on you," Thomas said, clasping Gareth's hand. "Bring us back the information we need to end this for good."

Gareth nodded, his grip firm. "We will. Stay strong and keep everyone safe."

Elara turned to Seraphina. "Are you ready for this?"

Seraphina's eyes were filled with determination. "I've been ready for this my whole life. Let's put an end to Valen's terror."

As the moon rose, casting a silver light over the village, the team assembled at the edge of the forest. Elara, Gareth, Seraphina, and a handful of the best scouts prepared to set out.

Gareth addressed the team, his voice low but resolute. "We move quickly and quietly. Our goal is to gather information and return safely. Trust in each other, and we'll succeed."

Elara added, "Remember, our strength lies in our unity. We'll face whatever comes together."

With final nods and words of encouragement, the team set off into the night, their figures soon swallowed by the darkness of the forest.

Beat 2: The Journey

The forest was dense and shadowed, the sounds of nocturnal creatures creating a symphony of night. The team moved with practiced silence, their senses heightened and alert. Every rustle of leaves and snap of a twig was scrutinized, their progress steady but cautious.

Elara led the way, her eyes scanning the path ahead. She signaled for a halt, turning to Seraphina. "Which way?"

Seraphina pointed to thc cast, her voice a whisper. "There's a hidden trail that leads to a vantage point overlooking the stronghold. It's not far, but we need to be careful."

Gareth moved closer, his presence a comforting assurance. "We're with you. Lead the way."

They continued, their movements synchronized and fluid. The forest seemed to close in around them, the canopy blocking out the moonlight, making their journey even more precarious.

After what felt like hours, Seraphina halted, holding up a hand. "We're close. Just over that ridge."

Elara and Gareth exchanged a glance, their hearts pounding with a mix of anticipation and caution. They followed Seraphina to the ridge, where they crouched low, peering through the underbrush.

Below them, a sprawling encampment spread out, dimly lit by fires and torches. Valen's stronghold. The sight was both daunting and illuminating.

Gareth's voice was barely audible. "There it is. Now we just need to gather as much information as possible."

Elara nodded, her eyes narrowing as she took in the layout of the camp. "We need to identify the key points—the command center, supply routes, and any weaknesses in their defenses."

Seraphina pointed to a large tent in the center. "That's where Valen holds his meetings. If we can get close enough, we might overhear something useful."

Elara turned to the team, her voice steady. "We split into pairs. Gather what you can and meet back here in one hour. Be careful."

As they moved into position, the weight of their mission settled over them. They were deep in enemy territory, but their determination to protect their home and end Valen's reign of terror drove them forward.

Elara and Gareth moved together, their silent communication and trust making them an effective team. They observed the guards' patterns, noted the locations of key structures, and listened for any valuable information.

After an hour, they regrouped at the ridge, each pair having gathered crucial intelligence. Seraphina, her eyes shining with excitement and fear, whispered, "We've got what we need. Let's get out of here before they notice us."

Gareth nodded, his expression tense. "Move quickly and quietly. We can't afford any mistakes now."

As they began their retreat, Elara felt a surge of hope. They had the information they needed to strike at Valen's heart. The journey back to the village was fraught with tension, but their unity and resolve kept them focused.

By dawn, they emerged from the forest, weary but triumphant. The village greeted them with a mixture of relief and anticipation. Elara and Gareth knew the hardest part was yet to come, but with the knowledge they had gained, they were ready to lead their people to victory. Together, they would face the coming storm and build a future of peace and prosperity.

The dawn light filtered through the trees as Elara, Gareth, and their team returned to the village. The villagers, already awake and bustling with activity, paused to greet them, their faces filled with anticipation and hope. Elder Brynn and the council gathered quickly, eager to hear the news.

Elara wasted no time. "We found Valen's stronghold. It's heavily fortified, but we've gathered valuable information about their defenses and the layout of the camp."

Gareth continued, "We need to strike quickly and decisively. Valen's forces are still regrouping, but they won't stay disorganized for long."

Elder Brynn's eyes were filled with concern but also resolve. "What's our plan?"

Seraphina stepped forward, her voice steady. "The camp is vulnerable in several key areas. If we can disrupt their supply lines and take out their command center, we can create enough chaos to dismantle their forces."

Maren nodded thoughtfully. "We'll need to divide our forces. A smaller team to infiltrate and cause disruption, and the main force to attack once the chaos begins."

Thomas added, "We should also set traps and ambush points along their retreat routes. If they try to flee, we'll be ready."

Elara's gaze swept over the gathered leaders. "We've faced Valen before, and we've won. This time, we end his threat for good. Let's divide into teams and go over the specifics."

As they moved to a large map spread out on a table, the air was filled with a mix of tension and determination. The leaders huddled together, discussing strategies and allocating tasks.

"Elara, you'll lead the infiltration team," Maren said, her voice firm. "Your knowledge of their camp is crucial."

Gareth nodded. "I'll command the main force. We'll be ready to strike as soon as the signal is given."

Seraphina pointed to the supply routes marked on the map. "We'll need to hit these points hard and fast. Disrupt their supplies, and their defenses will weaken."

Thomas added, "I'll set up the ambush points. We'll catch any fleeing raiders and make sure they can't regroup."

Elder Brynn's voice was filled with solemn pride. "You all know what's at stake. Fight with courage and unity. Our future depends on it."

As the meeting adjourned, Elara and Gareth took a moment to address the gathered fighters. The sense of purpose and resolve was palpable.

"We've trained for this," Elara said, her voice carrying across the square. "We know our strengths, and we know our enemy's weaknesses. Trust in each other and stay focused."

Gareth's eyes met each fighter's gaze, his voice steady. "This is our chance to end Valen's threat once and for all. We fight for our home, our families, and our future. Together, we are unstoppable."

The fighters responded with a cheer, their spirits lifted by the confidence and determination of their leaders. As the teams prepared for the upcoming battle, Elara and Gareth moved among them, offering words of encouragement and final instructions.

"We move out at dusk," Gareth said, his eyes meeting Elara's. "Rest and prepare. We'll need every ounce of strength and resolve."

Elara nodded, her heart filled with a mix of anticipation and determination. "We're ready. Let's bring an end to this."

As dusk fell, the village was a hive of activity, the final preparations for the assault in full swing. The fighters gathered their weapons, checked their gear, and steeled themselves for the battle ahead. Elara, Gareth, and Seraphina led the infiltration team, moving swiftly and silently through the forest.

The air was thick with tension as they approached Valen's stronghold. The camp was eerily quiet, the fires casting long shadows across the ground. Elara signaled for the team to halt, her eyes scanning the perimeter.

"Remember, our goal is to create chaos," she whispered. "Hit the supply points first, then the command center. Move quickly and stay hidden."

Seraphina nodded, her eyes sharp with focus. "I'll lead a group to the main supply tent. We'll create a distraction there."

Gareth's voice was low but firm. "We'll take out the guards at the command center. Once we signal, the main force will attack."

As they moved into position, the tension was palpable. Every sound seemed amplified in the silence of the night. Elara's heart pounded in her chest, but her resolve was unshaken.

Seraphina's group moved to the supply tent, positioning themselves for a swift attack. With a nod from Seraphina, they struck, disabling guards and setting fire to the supplies. The sudden blaze lit up the camp, shouts of alarm echoing through the night.

At the same time, Elara and Gareth led their team to the command center. They moved with deadly precision, taking out guards and creating chaos among Valen's forces. Gareth signaled to the main force, who stormed the camp, catching the disorganized raiders off guard.

"For the village!" Gareth shouted, his voice a rallying cry.

The battle erupted into a flurry of movement and sound. Fighters clashed, the air filled with the clang of steel and the cries of combat. Elara fought with fierce determination, her sword a blur as she cut through the enemy ranks.

"We've got them!" Seraphina shouted, her voice filled with triumph. "Keep pushing!"

The raiders, disoriented and demoralized, began to fall back. Elara and Gareth pressed their advantage, their fighters moving in to secure key positions. The tide of battle was turning in their favor.

As the camp fell into chaos, Valen appeared, his face twisted with rage. He charged toward Elara, his sword raised. Elara met his attack head-on, their blades clashing with a resounding clang.

"You've lost, Valen," Elara said, her voice steady despite the intensity of the battle.

Valen sneered. "This isn't over. I'll see your village burn before I'm done."

Gareth moved to flank Valen, his eyes blazing with determination. "Not today."

Together, Elara and Gareth fought with a seamless unity, their movements synchronized and precise. Valen's attacks were fierce, but their bond and resolve were stronger. With a final, decisive strike, Elara disarmed Valen, her blade at his throat.

"It's over," she said, her voice filled with finality.

Valen glared at her, his eyes filled with hate. "You may have won this battle, but you'll never be rid of me."

Gareth stepped forward, his expression cold. "We'll see about that."

With Valen subdued, the remaining raiders either fled or surrendered. The camp fell silent, the fires dying down as the first light of dawn began to break. The village fighters gathered, their faces filled with relief and triumph.

"We did it," Seraphina said, her voice breathless with exhaustion and joy. "We've won."

Elara and Gareth stood together, their hearts swelling with pride. "This victory is ours," Elara said, her voice carrying across the camp. "We fought with courage and unity, and we prevailed."

Gareth nodded, his eyes meeting Elara's. "We've secured our future. Together, we can face anything."

As the sun rose, casting a golden light over the battlefield, the village fighters cheered, their voices ringing out in celebration. Elara and Gareth knew that the road ahead would still have its challenges, but with their unity and resolve, they were ready to face whatever came next.

Together, they had built a legacy of strength, courage, and enduring hope. And together, they would continue to lead their people into a future of peace and prosperity.

Chapter 19
Rebuilding Trust

The victory over Valen's forces brought a much-needed sense of relief to the village, but Elara and Gareth knew that the real work was just beginning. The allied villages had gathered for a council meeting to discuss the next steps. The meeting hall buzzed with the energy of leaders eager to forge a new path forward.

Elder Brynn opened the meeting, his voice steady but filled with urgency. "We've secured a great victory, but we must ensure lasting peace. We need to rebuild, strengthen our defenses, and continue to foster the unity that brought us here."

Thomas leaned forward, his eyes reflecting the seriousness of the situation. "Our defenses held, but we need to fortify them further. We can't afford to be caught off guard again."

Maren nodded in agreement. "The western village is prepared to send resources and builders to help with the reconstruction. We should focus on strategic points that were vulnerable during the last attack."

Elara spoke up, her voice calm but firm. "We also need to address the wounds left by Valen's reign. Many villages suffered losses, and we must provide support for the families affected. Unity isn't just about defense; it's about caring for each other."

Gareth added, "We should set up a network to share resources and information more efficiently. Regular meetings of this council will ensure that we stay coordinated and ready for any future threats."

Anara, representing the northern villages, raised her hand. "I propose that we establish a communication network using signal fires and messengers. It worked during the battle, and it can be refined for peacetime coordination."

Seraphina, now a trusted advisor, spoke from the back of the room. "We also need to root out any remaining supporters of Valen. They may try to regroup or incite unrest. Our scouts should remain vigilant."

Maren turned to Seraphina, her expression thoughtful. "You've proven your loyalty, Seraphina. Your knowledge of Valen's tactics has been invaluable. What do you suggest for maintaining security?"

Seraphina stood, her voice steady and confident. "We need to keep the pressure on. Regular patrols, surprise inspections of known hideouts, and continued intelligence gathering. We can't let our guard down."

Elder Brynn nodded approvingly. "Your suggestions are sound. We must balance vigilance with rebuilding. Our people need to see progress and feel safe."

Thomas looked around the room, his gaze settling on each leader. "We should also celebrate our victory and honor those who fought bravely. A public ceremony will strengthen our bonds and remind everyone of what we've achieved together."

Elara smiled, feeling the unity and resolve in the room. "Agreed. Let's plan a ceremony to honor our fighters and renew our commitment to each other. It will be a powerful symbol of our unity."

Gareth's eyes met Elara's, his expression filled with pride and determination. "We've come a long way, but this is just the beginning. Together, we'll build a future of peace and prosperity."

The council members nodded in agreement, their faces reflecting the hope and determination that had carried them through the darkest times. Plans were made, resources allocated, and roles assigned, all with a shared vision of a united and resilient future.

As the meeting adjourned, Elara and Gareth stayed behind to discuss the final details with Elder Brynn. "We've achieved so much," Elara said softly. "But there's still so much to do."

Brynn's eyes were filled with warmth and wisdom. "You've shown incredible leadership and courage. The village is stronger because of you. Keep guiding us with that same strength, and we'll continue to thrive."

Gareth placed a hand on Elara's shoulder. "We'll do whatever it takes. For our people, and for the future we're building together."

The day of the ceremony dawned bright and clear, a perfect backdrop for the celebration of unity and victory. The village square was transformed with banners, flowers, and a large platform where the leaders would speak. Villagers from all the allied communities gathered, their faces filled with anticipation and pride.

Elara and Gareth stood at the center of the platform, flanked by the other leaders. Elder Brynn began the ceremony, his voice carrying across the square. "Today, we honor the bravery and sacrifice of those who fought to protect our homes. We celebrate our unity and look forward to a future of peace and cooperation."

Thomas stepped forward, his voice strong. "Our victory was possible because of our unity. We stood together, fought together, and now we rebuild together. This is just the beginning."

Maren addressed the crowd next, her eyes shining with pride. "The western village pledges to support the reconstruction efforts. We'll provide builders, resources, and whatever else is needed to strengthen our defenses and our community."

Anara added, "The northern villages are committed to maintaining our alliance. We'll continue to share resources and information, ensuring that we remain strong and united."

Seraphina, who had earned the trust and respect of the villagers, spoke last. "I stand before you as proof that even those who were once enemies can become allies. Together, we can overcome any threat and build a future of peace."

Elara took a deep breath, her heart swelling with pride and hope. She stepped forward, her voice filled with emotion. "This victory belongs to all of us. We've shown that through unity and determination, we can achieve anything. Let's continue to stand together, support each other, and build a future where peace and prosperity reign."

Gareth joined her, his voice echoing her sentiment. "We've faced darkness and emerged stronger. Our unity is our greatest strength. Together, we will protect our home and ensure a bright future for generations to come."

The crowd erupted in cheers, their voices a powerful affirmation of their collective resolve. The ceremony continued with music, dancing, and the sharing of food, a celebration of their hard-won victory and the bonds that had been forged in the fires of struggle.

As the sun set, casting a warm glow over the village, Elara and Gareth walked through the square, speaking with villagers and leaders, their hearts filled with hope and determination. They knew that the road ahead would still have its challenges, but with their unity and unwavering commitment, they were ready to face whatever came next.

Together, they had built a legacy of strength, courage, and enduring hope. And together, they would continue to lead their people into a future of peace and prosperity, always standing united against any threat.

The village square was abuzz with the sounds of celebration. The festival of renewal, an idea brought forth by Maren and supported by the entire council, was in full swing. Stalls lined the square, filled with goods from the allied villages, showcasing their unity and shared prosperity. Music filled the air, and children laughed as they played games, the tension of recent battles a distant memory.

Elara and Gareth walked through the square, their presence a beacon of reassurance and strength. They stopped at a stall where villagers from the northern territories displayed their crafts.

Anara greeted them with a broad smile. "Elara, Gareth, it's good to see you both enjoying the festival. The people needed this."

Elara nodded, her eyes bright with happiness. "It's wonderful to see everyone coming together like this. It's a testament to our unity and resilience."

Gareth added, "It also shows that we can build a future filled with joy and prosperity. This festival is a symbol of our renewed strength."

As they moved on, they encountered Thomas, who was overseeing a group of children learning to carve wood. His usually stern face was softened with a rare smile.

"Thomas, it's great to see you in such high spirits," Elara remarked.

Thomas chuckled. "These kids remind me of why we fight so hard. They deserve to grow up in a world free from fear."

Gareth nodded, his expression thoughtful. "And we're making that world a reality. Step by step."

Near the center of the square, they found Elder Brynn speaking with Seraphina. The two were deep in conversation but paused to greet Elara and Gareth.

"Elder Brynn, Seraphina," Gareth said, his voice warm. "How are you finding the festival?"

Brynn smiled, his eyes twinkling with contentment. "It's a beautiful sight. Our people celebrating together, free from the shadow of fear. It's everything we've worked for."

Seraphina's expression was more reflective. "It's a reminder of what we've achieved and what we still need to protect. The bonds we've forged here are our greatest strength."

Elara placed a hand on Seraphina's shoulder. "You've become an integral part of our community, Seraphina. Your insights and bravery have been invaluable."

Seraphina's eyes softened with gratitude. "Thank you, Elara. I'm proud to be part of this."

As they continued their walk, Elara spotted a group of villagers from the western territories. Maren was among them, sharing a hearty laugh.

"Maren!" Elara called, waving.

Maren turned, her smile wide. "Elara, Gareth! Come join us. We were just discussing the future projects to strengthen our defenses and improve our trade routes."

Elara and Gareth joined the group, the conversation flowing easily. Ideas were exchanged about improving the infrastructure and ensuring that each village had what it needed to thrive.

Maren's enthusiasm was infectious. "We're planning a new trade route that will make it easier to share resources. It's a big project, but with everyone's help, we can make it happen."

Gareth nodded, his eyes shining with determination. "This is exactly what we need. Continued cooperation and mutual support. Together, we can achieve anything."

As the festival continued into the evening, Elara and Gareth took a moment to stand at the edge of the square, looking out over the joyful scene. The village was alive with light and laughter, the air filled with the promise of a bright future.

"We've come so far," Elara said softly, her voice filled with emotion.

Gareth's hand found hers, their fingers intertwining. "And we have so much more to look forward to. Together, we've built something truly remarkable."

The festival began to wind down as the evening wore on, but the sense of unity and celebration lingered in the air. The leaders of the allied villages gathered around a large bonfire, their faces illuminated by the dancing flames. Elara and Gareth stood with them, the warmth of the fire a comforting presence.

Elder Brynn raised his voice, calling for attention. "Tonight, we celebrate not only our victory but the bonds that have strengthened our communities. Let us share our thoughts and hopes for the future."

Thomas was the first to speak, his voice filled with conviction. "Our unity has brought us through the darkest times. Let's continue to build on this foundation, ensuring that every village thrives and that we stand ready to face any challenge together."

Maren added, "The projects we've discussed today will benefit all our villages. By improving our trade routes and fortifying our defenses, we ensure that no village stands alone."

Anara's voice was filled with warmth and optimism. "The northern villages are committed to this alliance. We'll continue to share our resources and knowledge, strengthening our bonds and ensuring our collective security."

Seraphina spoke next, her tone reflective. "I've seen the darkness that can arise when communities are divided. What we have here is precious. We must nurture it and protect it with all our strength."

Elara and Gareth shared a look before Gareth stepped forward. "We've seen firsthand what we can achieve when we stand together. This festival is a celebration of our unity and our strength. Let's pledge to continue working together, supporting each other, and building a future of peace and prosperity."

Elara nodded, her voice carrying a quiet strength. "Our unity is our greatest weapon against any threat. Let's honor the bonds we've forged and ensure that they grow stronger with each passing day."

The leaders nodded in agreement, their faces reflecting the shared resolve. The bonfire crackled, sending sparks into the night sky, a symbol of their enduring spirit.

As the conversation continued, plans were made for future council meetings, trade agreements, and joint training exercises. The sense of camaraderie was palpable, each leader committed to the vision of a united and prosperous future.

Later, as the fire began to die down, Elara and Gareth took a moment to reflect on the day's events. They walked through the quieting village, the laughter and music of the festival fading into the night.

"We've achieved so much," Elara said softly, her eyes reflecting the flickering light of the remaining fires. "But there's always more to do."

Gareth squeezed her hand, his voice filled with determination. "And we'll do it together. This is just the beginning. Our unity, our commitment to each other, will carry us forward."

They paused at the edge of the village, looking out over the peaceful scene. The stars shone brightly above, a reminder of the vast possibilities that lay ahead.

"We've built something truly remarkable," Elara said, her voice filled with pride and hope. "And together, we'll continue to build a future of peace and prosperity."

Gareth nodded, his heart swelling with love and determination. "Together, always."

As they stood there, side by side, the future stretched out before them, filled with promise and potential. They had faced incredible challenges and emerged stronger for it. With their unity and unwavering commitment, they knew they could overcome any obstacle and build a legacy of strength, courage, and enduring hope.

Together, they were ready to face whatever came next, confident in the bonds they had forged and the community they had built. The journey ahead would be filled with challenges, but also with opportunities to grow and thrive. And they would face it all, together.

Chapter 20
Paths Forward

The village had settled into a peaceful rhythm, the harmony of daily life a testament to the resilience and unity of the people. However, tranquility was often a prelude to new challenges. One crisp morning, an unfamiliar figure approached the village gates. The guards, alert but cautious, halted the visitor and sent for Elara and Gareth.

Elara and Gareth arrived promptly, their eyes narrowing as they assessed the stranger. He was a tall man, dressed in travel-worn clothes, with an air of quiet confidence.

"Who are you?" Elara asked, her voice steady but guarded.

The man bowed slightly. "My name is Kael. I come from the southern territories. I've traveled far to seek an audience with the leaders of this village."

Gareth's eyes remained skeptical. "What brings you here, Kael?"

Kael met Gareth's gaze evenly. "I've heard of your victory against Valen and the unity you've forged among the allied villages. My people face a similar threat, and I believe we can learn from your example."

Elara's expression softened slightly, but her caution remained. "What threat do your people face?"

Kael sighed, his eyes reflecting a mix of weariness and determination. "A warlord named Thorne has been terrorizing our lands. He's ruthless, and his forces are growing. We've tried to resist, but we lack the unity and strength you've shown. I'm here to request your help and to offer an alliance."

The mention of another warlord caused a murmur among the gathered villagers. Elara glanced at Gareth, who nodded slightly.

"Let's discuss this further inside," Elara said, gesturing towards the meeting hall. "We need to understand the full scope of the situation."

Inside the hall, Elder Brynn, Thomas, Maren, Anara, and Seraphina joined Elara and Gareth, listening intently as Kael recounted the struggles of his people.

"Thorne is cunning and brutal," Kael explained. "He's taken control of several key territories, and his influence is spreading. We've managed to hold him off so far, but we're losing ground. Our only hope is to unite, as you have done."

Thomas leaned forward, his expression serious. "We've faced similar challenges, and we know the importance of unity. But we need to understand more about Thorne's tactics and forces before we can commit to anything."

Kael nodded. "I understand. I've brought maps and information on his strongholds and movements. I'm willing to share everything I know."

Maren spoke up, her voice thoughtful. "An alliance could benefit both our peoples. We've seen the strength that comes from working together. But we need to assess the risks and ensure we're prepared for another conflict."

Anara added, "We should send scouts to verify Kael's information and gather more intelligence. If Thorne is as dangerous as he says, we need to be ready."

Elder Brynn's eyes were filled with wisdom and concern. "We must weigh our options carefully. Unity is our strength, but we must ensure that we don't overextend ourselves."

Seraphina, who had been quietly listening, finally spoke. "We've learned a lot from our battles with Valen. If we decide to help, we need to apply those lessons and plan strategically. This won't be easy, but it could strengthen our alliances and bring greater peace to the region."

Elara and Gareth exchanged a look, their unspoken communication clear. They had faced many challenges together, and this was another that required careful consideration and unified action.

"We'll discuss this with the council and make a decision soon," Elara said, turning to Kael. "Thank you for bringing this to our attention. We'll do what we can to help."

Kael bowed again, gratitude evident in his eyes. "Thank you. My people will be forever grateful for your support."

As Kael left the meeting hall, the leaders remained to discuss the situation further. The weight of their decision was heavy, but their commitment to unity and protection of the innocent was unwavering.

"We need to be cautious but decisive," Gareth said, his voice filled with resolve. "This could be an opportunity to strengthen our alliances and bring peace to more regions."

Elara nodded, her mind racing with possibilities. "Let's prepare our scouts and gather as much information as we can. We'll need a clear picture before we move forward."

The council agreed, their faces reflecting the seriousness of the task ahead. The journey to lasting peace was far from over, but with unity and determination, they were ready to face whatever challenges lay ahead.

The next few days were a flurry of activity as scouts were dispatched to the southern territories to verify Kael's information. The council reconvened in the meeting hall, their expressions reflecting a mix of anticipation and apprehension.

Thomas began the meeting, his voice steady. "Our scouts have returned with detailed reports. Thorne's forces are indeed as formidable as Kael described. They're well-organized and heavily armed, but they also have vulnerabilities we can exploit."

Maren nodded. "We've identified key supply routes and weak points in their defenses. If we strike strategically, we can significantly weaken Thorne's hold on the region."

Anara added, "The northern villages are prepared to send fighters and resources. We've faced similar threats, and we're ready to stand with the southern territories."

Elder Brynn's eyes were thoughtful. "We must consider the impact on our own defenses. We can't afford to leave ourselves vulnerable."

Seraphina spoke, her voice filled with determination. "We've learned the importance of planning and unity. If we coordinate our efforts, we can support Kael's people without compromising our own security."

Elara and Gareth listened intently, weighing the options. The decision was complex, but the stakes were clear. Elara finally spoke, her voice resolute. "We've always stood for unity and protection of the innocent. We can't turn our backs on those in need."

Gareth nodded in agreement. "We'll proceed with caution, but we must act. Let's finalize our plans and prepare for the mission."

The council members exchanged determined looks, their resolve solidifying. They spent the next hours detailing strategies, allocating resources, and ensuring that every aspect of the mission was covered.

As the meeting concluded, Elder Brynn addressed the council. "We've made our decision. Now we must follow through with the same unity and strength that has brought us this far. Together, we will face this new challenge and emerge stronger."

Elara and Gareth left the meeting hall, their minds filled with the weight of their decision. They walked through the village, speaking with the people and preparing them for the tasks ahead.

"We've faced so much together," Elara said softly. "And we'll continue to face whatever comes, side by side."

Gareth squeezed her hand, his voice filled with confidence. "Together, we can achieve anything. This is just another step in our journey."

The village buzzed with activity as preparations for the mission began. The sense of unity and purpose was palpable, each person committed to the shared goal of peace and protection.

Elara and Gareth stood at the center of it all, their leadership a beacon of hope and strength. They had faced countless challenges and emerged victorious, and they were ready to lead their people into this new chapter with the same unwavering resolve.

As the sun set, casting a warm glow over the village, Elara and Gareth looked out over their community. They had built something remarkable, and with their unity and determination, they would continue to build a future of peace and prosperity for all.

Together, they were unstoppable, ready to face whatever challenges lay ahead and build a legacy of strength, courage, and enduring hope.

The day of departure loomed closer, and the village was abuzz with preparations. The meeting hall was filled with the leaders and key fighters, their faces reflecting a mix of determination and apprehension. Elara and Gareth stood at the head of the room, ready to finalize the strategy for aiding the southern territories.

Elder Brynn called for order, his voice calm yet commanding. "We've gathered the intelligence and resources needed for this mission. Now, let's finalize our strategy and ensure everyone knows their roles."

Thomas stepped forward, a map spread out before him. "Our scouts have identified the key vulnerabilities in Thorne's defenses. We'll strike these points simultaneously to maximize our impact."

Maren nodded, pointing to the map. "We'll need to divide our forces into three main groups. The first group will target the supply lines, cutting off their resources. The second group will create a diversion to draw Thorne's forces away from the main stronghold. The third group, led by Gareth and Elara, will infiltrate the stronghold and take out Thorne's command center."

Anara's eyes were filled with resolve. "The northern villages will provide additional fighters and resources for the first and second groups. We'll coordinate our efforts to ensure precise timing."

Seraphina spoke next, her voice steady. "I'll lead a team of scouts to monitor Thorne's movements and relay information back to the main force. We need to stay one step ahead."

Gareth addressed the group, his voice strong and confident. "Communication will be crucial. We'll use signal fires and messengers to coordinate our attacks. Remember, our strength lies in our unity. Trust in each other and in the plan."

Elara added, her gaze sweeping over the gathered fighters. "We've faced great challenges before and emerged victorious. This mission is no different. We fight for the future of our allies and for the peace we've worked so hard to build."

Elder Brynn's eyes were filled with wisdom and pride. "You've all shown remarkable courage and resilience. Go with the knowledge that you carry the hopes and strength of our people. Return victorious."

As the meeting adjourned, the leaders and fighters dispersed to make final preparations. Elara and Gareth moved among them, offering words of encouragement and ensuring that every detail was covered.

Elara approached Seraphina, who was reviewing the scout reports. "Seraphina, your insights have been invaluable. Are you ready for this mission?"

Seraphina's eyes were steady. "I am. We've planned carefully, and we're ready for whatever comes. I won't let you down."

Gareth joined them, his expression serious but supportive. "We're all in this together. Just remember, stick to the plan and stay alert."

Thomas approached, a determined look on his face. "The fighters are ready. We'll hit them hard and fast, just as we planned."

Maren added, "Our people know what's at stake. We'll do whatever it takes to ensure victory."

Elara and Gareth shared a look, their unspoken bond of trust and resolve clear. "We move out at dawn," Elara said. "Get some rest and be ready."

The night passed with an air of tense anticipation. As dawn broke, the village was a hive of activity, the fighters assembling and final checks being made. Elara and Gareth stood at the forefront, their presence a source of strength for their people.

Gareth's voice rang out, carrying across the assembled fighters. "This is it. We fight not just for ourselves, but for our allies and for the future of our people. Let's show Thorne the power of our unity."

Elara's voice followed, filled with determination. "Stay focused, stay strong, and trust in each other. Together, we will prevail."

With final nods and words of encouragement, the groups set off, each heading towards their designated targets. The mission to aid the southern territories and defeat Thorne had begun.

The march through the forest was swift and silent, the fighters moving with practiced precision. Elara and Gareth led the infiltration team, their senses heightened as they approached Thorne's stronghold. The tension was palpable, every rustle of leaves and snap of twigs magnified in the silence.

Seraphina, leading the scouts, returned with updates. "Thorne's forces are spread thin, just as we anticipated. The diversions are working."

Gareth nodded. "Good. Everyone knows their roles. Let's move into position."

As they neared the stronghold, Elara signaled for the team to halt. "Remember, our goal is to create enough chaos to take down Thorne's command. Move swiftly and stay alert."

The team moved into position, ready to strike. The first group attacked the supply lines, disabling guards and setting fire to supplies. Shouts of alarm echoed through the camp, drawing Thorne's forces away from the main stronghold.

Thomas led the diversionary attack, his fighters clashing with Thorne's men in a fierce battle. "Hold the line!" he shouted, his voice a rallying cry. "We need to buy Elara and Gareth time!"

Maren's group targeted the flanks, cutting off reinforcements and creating confusion among the enemy ranks. "Keep pushing!" she urged her fighters. "We've got them on the run!"

Inside the stronghold, Elara and Gareth moved with deadly precision, taking out guards and securing key positions. They reached the command center, where Thorne awaited, flanked by his most loyal fighters.

"So, you've come to die," Thorne sneered, his eyes filled with malice.

Elara stepped forward, her sword at the ready. "No, Thorne. We've come to end your reign of terror."

Gareth's voice was cold and steady. "Surrender now, and we may show mercy."

Thorne laughed, a harsh, grating sound. "Mercy is for the weak. I will crush you all."

The battle that ensued was fierce and chaotic. Elara and Gareth fought side by side, their movements synchronized and precise. Thorne's fighters were skilled, but they were no match for the unity and determination of Elara and Gareth's team.

As the battle raged, Seraphina and her scouts provided crucial updates, ensuring that the main force remained coordinated. "They're trying to regroup at the eastern gate!" she shouted.

Gareth signaled to his team. "Cut them off! Don't let them escape!"

Elara faced Thorne, their swords clashing with a resounding ring. "It's over, Thorne," she said, her voice filled with conviction. "You've lost."

Thorne's eyes blazed with fury. "I will never be defeated by the likes of you!"

With a final, decisive strike, Elara disarmed Thorne, her sword at his throat. "Yield," she commanded.

Thorne glared at her, his defiance unbroken. "Do your worst."

Gareth stepped forward, his expression grim. "You will answer for your crimes."

As Thorne's remaining forces surrendered or fled, the battle came to an end. The stronghold was secured, and the fighters gathered, their faces reflecting a mix of exhaustion and triumph.

Elara addressed the gathered fighters, her voice carrying across the courtyard. "We've won a great victory today. Through our unity and strength, we've defeated a formidable enemy. This is a testament to what we can achieve together."

Gareth added, his voice filled with pride. "We fought for our allies, and we fought for peace. Let this victory be a reminder of our resolve and our commitment to each other."

The fighters cheered, their voices echoing through the stronghold. The sense of unity and accomplishment was palpable, each person proud of their contribution to the victory.

As the sun set, casting a warm glow over the battlefield, Elara and Gareth stood together, their hearts filled with hope and determination. They had faced another great challenge and emerged victorious, their bond and their community stronger than ever.

Together, they would continue to lead their people into a future of peace and prosperity, ready to face whatever challenges lay ahead with the same unwavering resolve.

Chapter 21
New Horizons

The village buzzed with the energy of rebuilding and renewal. The victory over Thorne had not only secured peace for their own territories but also strengthened their alliances. Elara and Gareth were at the heart of these efforts, their leadership inspiring hope and determination.

One morning, as they were discussing plans for new trade routes with Maren and Thomas, a messenger arrived with urgent news. Elder Brynn called for a meeting in the hall, and soon, the key leaders were gathered, curious and alert.

Elder Brynn addressed them, his voice grave but controlled. "We've received a message from the southern territories. They're requesting our presence for an urgent council meeting."

Maren frowned. "What's the nature of this urgency?"

Elder Brynn glanced at the message in his hands. "It appears they want to discuss a proposal for a more permanent alliance, something beyond our current agreements."

Thomas leaned back, his eyes narrowing thoughtfully. "A permanent alliance? This could mean sharing resources, military support, and even governance. It's a significant commitment."

Elara and Gareth exchanged a look. "It's a big step," Elara said. "But if it strengthens our region and ensures lasting peace, it's worth considering."

Gareth nodded. "Agreed. We need to hear them out. Understanding their vision and intentions will help us make an informed decision."

Anara, representing the northern villages, spoke up. "Our people have seen the benefits of our current alliances. A more permanent structure could solidify those gains and provide a stronger front against any future threats."

Seraphina added, "We've proven that we can work together effectively. A formal alliance could also facilitate better communication and resource sharing."

Elder Brynn's eyes scanned the room, noting the consensus. "Very well. We will attend the council meeting. Elara, Gareth, you will lead our delegation."

Elara nodded, her expression resolute. "We'll prepare to leave immediately. This is an opportunity to shape the future of our region."

As the leaders dispersed to make preparations, Elara and Gareth walked through the village, discussing the implications of the proposal. "A permanent alliance would mean deeper integration," Gareth said, his voice thoughtful. "It's a significant change."

Elara nodded, her mind racing with possibilities. "But it could also mean greater stability and security for all our people. We've seen how effective our unity can be in times of crisis."

Later that day, as they prepared for the journey, Seraphina approached them. "I'd like to accompany you," she said. "My insights into Thorne's tactics might be useful, and I believe in the importance of this alliance."

Elara smiled. "We'd be glad to have you with us. Your perspective will be valuable."

Gareth agreed. "Your presence strengthens our delegation. Let's make sure we're ready for any eventuality."

As the small delegation set out, the weight of their mission was palpable. They traveled swiftly, the journey marked by discussions about the potential alliance and its benefits.

Upon arriving in the southern territories, they were greeted by Kael and other leaders. The council meeting was held in a large hall, the atmosphere charged with anticipation and hope.

Kael began the meeting, his voice filled with urgency and conviction. "We've seen the strength of our combined forces and the benefits of our cooperation. But Thorne's defeat is just the beginning. We face numerous challenges that require a united and strategic approach."

A southern leader, Marek, spoke up. "We propose a permanent alliance that encompasses military support, resource sharing, and a unified council to oversee regional governance. This will ensure that we can respond swiftly and effectively to any threats."

Elara listened intently, her mind weighing the implications. "We've seen how powerful unity can be. But we need to understand the specifics of this proposal and ensure that it benefits all parties fairly."

Gareth added, "Transparency and mutual respect are crucial. We must build this alliance on a foundation of trust and shared goals."

As the discussion continued, the leaders shared their visions and concerns, each voice contributing to the shaping of a potential alliance. The sense of shared destiny was strong, and the commitment to peace and prosperity was evident.

The discussions stretched into the evening, the leaders working through the details of the proposed alliance. Elara and Gareth, along with the other leaders, examined every aspect to ensure it would be beneficial and fair.

As the meeting concluded, Kael stood and addressed the assembly. "We've made significant progress today. There's still much to discuss, but it's clear that we share a common vision for our future. Let's continue to work together to make this alliance a reality."

Elara nodded, her voice steady. "We'll return to our village and discuss these proposals with our council. It's important that everyone understands and agrees to the terms."

Gareth added, "We'll also gather input from our people. This alliance will affect all of us, and their voices must be heard."

As the delegation prepared to leave, Kael approached Elara and Gareth. "Thank you for your openness and willingness to consider this alliance. Your leadership has been an inspiration."

Elara smiled warmly. "We're all working towards the same goal: a future of peace and prosperity for our people."

Gareth nodded. "We'll continue to work together to achieve that goal. Let's keep the lines of communication open and ensure that we're all moving in the same direction."

The journey back to the village was filled with thoughtful discussions about the next steps. Elara and Gareth knew that building a permanent alliance would be challenging, but they were committed to seeing it through.

Back in the village, they convened a meeting with Elder Brynn, Thomas, Maren, Anara, and Seraphina to share the details of the proposal.

Elara began, "The southern territories have proposed a permanent alliance that includes military support, resource sharing, and a unified council. It's a significant step, but one that could bring lasting stability to our region."

Thomas leaned back, his expression thoughtful. "It's a bold move, but it could solidify our gains and ensure that we're better prepared for any future threats."

Maren added, "The benefits are clear, but we need to ensure that the terms are fair and that all parties are equally committed."

Anara nodded. "Our people need to understand what this alliance means for them. We should hold a series of meetings to gather their input and address any concerns."

Seraphina's voice was filled with conviction. "This alliance could be a powerful force for good. We've seen what we can achieve together.

Let's make sure we build it on a foundation of trust and mutual respect."

Elder Brynn's eyes shone with wisdom. "We've come a long way, but this is just the beginning. Let's proceed with care and ensure that we build something that will endure for generations."

Elara and Gareth looked around at their friends and allies, their hearts filled with hope and determination. They had faced many challenges together and emerged stronger for it. Now, they were ready to take the next step towards a future of peace and prosperity.

"We'll move forward together," Elara said, her voice filled with resolve. "This is our path, and we'll walk it side by side."

Gareth nodded, his gaze steady. "Together, always."

As they set about preparing for the next phase of their journey, the sense of unity and purpose was palpable. They were ready to face whatever challenges lay ahead, confident in their shared vision and unwavering commitment.

Upon their return to the village, Elara and Gareth immediately set about organizing a series of meetings to gather input from the villagers. The first of these meetings was held in the central square, where a large crowd had gathered, eager to hear about the proposed alliance and share their thoughts.

Elder Brynn stood at the front, his voice calm but carrying a sense of urgency. "We've been presented with an opportunity to form a permanent alliance with the southern territories. This alliance could bring lasting peace and prosperity, but it's a significant commitment. We want to hear your thoughts and concerns."

A murmur went through the crowd as people discussed among themselves. Elara and Gareth stepped forward, ready to address the villagers directly.

Elara began, her voice steady and reassuring. "We've seen the strength of our unity in defeating Valen and Thorne. This alliance is an extension of that unity, a way to ensure that our children and their children can live in peace."

Gareth added, "We understand that this is a big step. It will require changes and adjustments, but we believe it's a step worth taking. We're here to answer your questions and listen to your concerns."

A farmer named Doran raised his hand. "What does this alliancc mean for our daily lives? Will we be expected to send more fighters or resources?"

Elara nodded. "It's possible. The alliance will involve shared responsibilities, but it also means shared benefits. We'll have greater support in times of need and access to resources that can help us grow and thrive."

An elderly woman named Alina spoke next. "I've lived through many conflicts. How can we be sure this alliance will bring peace and not more wars?"

Gareth's expression was serious. "Peace is our goal, but we must always be prepared to defend it. This alliance is about creating a strong, united front that can deter threats and promote stability. We'll work closely with our allies to ensure that peace is maintained."

A young man named Jarek stepped forward, his voice filled with determination. "I'm willing to fight for our future, but I want to know that our voices will be heard. Will we have a say in the decisions made by this alliance?"

Elara smiled warmly. "Absolutely. The proposed council will include representatives from all allied territories. Your voices will be heard, and your concerns will be addressed. This alliance is built on mutual respect and shared decision-making."

Thomas, who had been standing quietly, stepped forward. "We've faced many challenges together and emerged stronger each time. This alliance is a chance to build on that strength, to create something lasting and powerful. We need to embrace this opportunity."

Maren added, "Our unity has been our greatest asset. This alliance will formalize that unity and ensure that we continue to stand strong together. We're not just joining forces; we're becoming a larger, more resilient community."

Anara's voice was filled with conviction. "We've seen what we can achieve when we work together. This alliance is a natural progression, a way to ensure that our future is secure and prosperous. Let's move forward with hope and determination."

As the villagers continued to ask questions and share their thoughts, Elara and Gareth listened carefully, addressing each concern with honesty and empathy. The sense of community and shared purpose was palpable, each person committed to the vision of a united and peaceful future.

By the end of the meeting, it was clear that while there were concerns, the overall sentiment was positive. The villagers were ready to embrace the opportunity for a stronger, more unified future.

The final meeting with the council was held the next day, bringing together the leaders of the allied villages to finalize the details of the proposed alliance. The atmosphere was one of determination and cautious optimism.

Elder Brynn opened the discussion. "We've heard from our people, and the sentiment is clear. There is strong support for moving forward with this alliance, but we must ensure that the terms are fair and beneficial for all parties."

Kael, representing the southern territories, spoke first. "We are committed to this alliance and are prepared to share resources and responsibilities equally. Our goal is to create a stable and prosperous region for all our people."

Marek added, "We propose a rotating leadership within the council to ensure that every territory has a voice and an opportunity to lead. This will promote fairness and shared governance."

Elara nodded. "That's a good start. We also need to establish clear guidelines for resource sharing and military support. Transparency and communication will be key to maintaining trust and cooperation."

Gareth addressed the council. "We suggest regular meetings, both in-person and via messengers, to ensure that we stay aligned and can address any issues promptly. Let's also create a system for conflict resolution, so any disputes can be handled fairly and efficiently."

Thomas leaned forward, his voice filled with determination. "Our strength lies in our unity. This alliance must be built on a foundation of mutual respect and shared goals. We're all in this together."

Maren added, "We should also focus on cultural exchange and mutual support. By learning from each other and sharing our traditions and knowledge, we can build stronger bonds and a more cohesive community."

Anara's eyes shone with conviction. "We've seen the benefits of our current cooperation. This alliance will formalize and strengthen those ties. Let's move forward with a clear vision and a commitment to each other's well-being."

Seraphina, who had been quietly observing, finally spoke. "I've seen the darkness that division and conflict can bring. This alliance is a chance to build something better, to create a future where our children can thrive in peace. Let's seize this opportunity with both hands."

Elder Brynn's voice was filled with wisdom and pride. "We've come a long way, but this is just the beginning. Let's finalize these terms and solidify our commitment to each other. Together, we can build a future of lasting peace and prosperity."

As the council members discussed and refined the terms of the alliance, the sense of unity and shared purpose grew stronger. By the end of the meeting, they had created a detailed agreement that outlined the responsibilities, benefits, and governance structure of the alliance.

Elara and Gareth stood together, their hearts filled with hope and determination. They had faced many challenges and emerged stronger for it. Now, they were ready to take the next step towards a future of peace and prosperity.

Elara addressed the council, her voice steady and resolute. "We've built something remarkable together. This alliance is a testament to our shared vision and commitment. Let's move forward with confidence and unity."

Gareth added, "Together, we are stronger. Together, we can achieve anything. Let's embrace this new beginning and work tirelessly to build a future of peace and prosperity for all our people."

The council members nodded in agreement, their faces reflecting the hope and determination that had carried them through the darkest times. They had laid the foundation for a brighter future, one built on unity, trust, and shared purpose.

As they left the meeting hall, the sense of accomplishment and anticipation was palpable. They were ready to face whatever challenges lay ahead, confident in their shared vision and unwavering commitment.

Together, they had built a legacy of strength, courage, and enduring hope. And together, they would continue to lead their people into a future of peace and prosperity, always standing united against any threat.

Chapter 22
Strengthening Ties

The village bustled with activity as preparations for the formal signing of the alliance agreement were underway. Flags representing each of the allied territories fluttered in the breeze, and a large stage had been erected in the village square. This ceremony was not only a symbolic act but also a practical step towards a united future.

Elara and Gareth moved through the crowd, ensuring everything was in order. Elder Brynn, Thomas, Maren, Anara, and Seraphina were also busy, each handling different aspects of the preparations.

Elder Brynn called them together for a final briefing. "This ceremony marks the beginning of a new era for our people. It's important that everything goes smoothly. Remember, this is not just about signing an agreement; it's about showing our commitment to unity and peace."

Thomas nodded, his eyes scanning the bustling square. "Security is tight, and we have contingencies in place. We're ready."

Maren added, "The villagers are excited but also a bit anxious. It's a big change, and it's our job to reassure them."

Anara's voice was filled with optimism. "We've come so far together. This is a chance to celebrate our unity and look forward to a bright future."

Seraphina, standing slightly apart, spoke up. "I'll keep an eye on the periphery. We've had no indications of trouble, but it's best to stay vigilant."

Elara looked around at her friends and allies, her heart swelling with pride and determination. "Let's make this a day to remember. Our unity has brought us here, and it will carry us forward."

Gareth squeezed her hand, his voice filled with conviction. "Together, we're unstoppable."

As the time for the ceremony approached, the village square filled with people. Leaders from the allied territories took their places on the stage, and a hush fell over the crowd as Elder Brynn stepped forward to speak.

"Friends and allies," he began, his voice carrying across the square. "Today, we come together to formalize an alliance that has already proven its strength in battle and in peace. This agreement is more than words on parchment; it is a commitment to each other, to our shared future, and to the peace and prosperity of our people."

Elara and Gareth stepped forward, holding the scroll that detailed the terms of the alliance. As they unrolled it, the other leaders gathered around, each prepared to add their signature.

Thomas was the first to sign, his expression serious but proud. "For the future of our people," he said, his voice strong.

Maren followed, her eyes shining with determination. "For unity and strength."

Anara's hand was steady as she added her name. "For peace and prosperity."

Seraphina signed last, her voice filled with conviction. "For a better tomorrow."

Elara and Gareth added their signatures, sealing the agreement. "For our children and for generations to come," Elara said, her voice filled with emotion.

Gareth's voice echoed hers. "Together, always."

As the leaders stepped back, the crowd erupted into cheers, their voices filled with hope and excitement. The sense of unity and shared purpose was palpable, each person committed to the vision of a united and peaceful future.

The ceremony flowed seamlessly into a grand celebration. Music filled the air, and tables laden with food and drink were set up around the square. Villagers and leaders mingled, sharing stories and laughter, the weight of past conflicts lifting with each passing moment.

Elara and Gareth moved through the crowd, speaking with villagers and leaders alike. They paused to talk with Kael, who had been instrumental in bringing about the alliance.

"This is a remarkable day," Kael said, his voice filled with emotion. "We've achieved something truly special here."

Elara smiled warmly. "It's the beginning of a new chapter for all of us. We've shown that unity is our greatest strength."

Gareth nodded in agreement. "And we'll continue to build on that strength, ensuring that our alliance remains strong and resilient."

As they continued to move through the crowd, they encountered Thomas, who was deep in conversation with a group of villagers. "We need to focus on the practical aspects of our alliance now," Thomas was saying. "Ensuring that our resource sharing and military support are well-coordinated."

Elara joined the conversation. "Thomas is right. The alliance is only as strong as the systems we put in place to support it. Let's make sure we follow through on our commitments."

Maren approached, her face lit with excitement. "We've already started planning joint training exercises and resource distribution. The western villages are eager to contribute and learn."

Anara added, "We're also looking at ways to integrate our cultural traditions, so we can learn from each other and build a more cohesive community."

Seraphina, who had been quietly observing, spoke up. "It's important that we keep communication open and transparent. Any misunderstandings could weaken our alliance. We need to address issues promptly and fairly."

Elder Brynn joined them, his expression one of pride and satisfaction. "You've all shown incredible leadership and vision. This alliance is a testament to your hard work and dedication. Let's ensure that it remains strong and vibrant."

Elara looked around at her friends and allies, her heart swelling with pride. "We've built something truly remarkable here. Let's continue to work together, to support each other, and to build a future of peace and prosperity."

Gareth's voice was filled with conviction. "Together, we can achieve anything. This alliance is just the beginning. Let's move forward with hope and determination."

As the evening wore on, the celebrations continued, filled with music, dancing, and laughter. The sense of unity and shared purpose was stronger than ever, each person committed to the vision of a united and peaceful future.

Elara and Gareth stood at the edge of the square, watching the celebrations with a sense of fulfillment and hope. They had faced countless challenges and emerged stronger for it. Now, they were ready to lead their people into a future of peace and prosperity.

"We've come so far," Elara said softly, her eyes reflecting the flickering lights of the celebration.

Gareth nodded, his hand finding hers. "And we have so much more to look forward to. Together, always."

As they stood there, side by side, the future stretched out before them, filled with promise and potential. They had built something remarkable, and with their unity and determination, they would continue to build a legacy of strength, courage, and enduring hope.

The celebration continued late into the night, but Elara and Gareth knew that the true test of the alliance would come in the days and months ahead. The next morning, they called for a village meeting to gather feedback and suggestions from the people, ensuring that every voice was heard as they moved forward.

The village square was filled with villagers and leaders from the allied territories, all eager to contribute to the discussion. Elder Brynn opened the meeting with a few words of encouragement, then handed the floor over to Elara and Gareth.

Elara stepped forward, her voice carrying the weight of their recent achievements and the promise of the future. "We've come together to celebrate our unity and the new alliance. But now, we must ensure that this alliance is strong and beneficial for everyone. We want to hear your thoughts, your concerns, and your ideas."

A young woman named Liora, who had been an active participant in the village defenses, raised her hand. "What steps are we taking to ensure that the resource sharing is fair and that no village feels neglected?"

Gareth nodded, appreciating the question. "We've set up a council with representatives from each village to oversee the distribution of resources. This council will meet regularly to address any issues and ensure that all needs are met fairly."

An older man named Thoren spoke next, his voice tinged with concern. "What about our defenses? Are we prepared if another threat arises?"

Thomas responded, his voice firm. "We're implementing joint training exercises and regular patrols across all territories. Our combined forces will be stronger and more prepared for any threats."

A young mother named Elena, holding her child, asked, "How will this alliance benefit our children? What future are we building for them?"

Maren's eyes softened as she answered. "This alliance is about more than just defense and resources. It's about creating a stable and prosperous future where our children can grow up in peace. We're also focusing on education and cultural exchange to enrich their lives."

Anara added, "We're planning events and programs that bring together people from all villages, fostering understanding and cooperation. Our children will benefit from a diverse and supportive community."

Seraphina, standing at the edge of the crowd, stepped forward. "Transparency and communication are key. We've learned from our past struggles that mistrust can lead to division. We need to keep the lines of communication open and address any concerns promptly."

A farmer named Doran voiced another concern. "What about our trade routes? How will this alliance affect our markets and the flow of goods?"

Elara smiled, glad to address a practical concern. "We're working on improving and expanding our trade routes to ensure that goods flow more freely between our villages. This will help boost our economies and ensure that everyone has access to what they need."

Gareth added, "We're also encouraging innovation and collaboration between our craftsmen and traders. By sharing knowledge and skills, we can all prosper."

Elder Brynn's eyes shone with pride as he listened to the engaged and thoughtful responses from the villagers. "You've all shown incredible wisdom and foresight. This is exactly what our alliance needs to thrive – the active participation and commitment of every member of our community."

As the meeting continued, more villagers voiced their ideas and concerns, each one adding to the collective vision of a united and prosperous future. The sense of community and shared purpose was palpable, each person committed to the success of the alliance.

With the meeting drawing to a close, Elara and Gareth took a moment to reflect on the discussions. The feedback from the villagers had been invaluable, providing a clear picture of the hopes and concerns that would shape the future of the alliance.

Elara addressed the crowd once more, her voice filled with gratitude and determination. "Thank you all for your contributions. Your voices are the foundation of our alliance. Together, we will build a future that honors our shared values and aspirations."

Gareth's voice was steady and confident. "We've achieved so much already, but this is just the beginning. Let's continue to work together, to support each other, and to ensure that our alliance remains strong and vibrant."

The villagers responded with cheers and applause, their spirits lifted by the sense of unity and shared purpose. As the crowd began to disperse, Elara and Gareth remained in the square, talking with small groups and addressing individual concerns.

Elder Brynn joined them, his expression one of quiet satisfaction. "You've done well, both of you. The strength of our alliance lies in the trust and commitment of our people. And you've fostered that trust beautifully."

Elara smiled, feeling the weight of their responsibilities but also the support of their community. "We've all worked hard to get here. And we'll continue to work hard to ensure that this alliance thrives."

Gareth nodded, his gaze steady. "Together, we can face whatever challenges come our way. This alliance is a testament to our unity and our shared vision for the future."

As the sun set, casting a warm glow over the village, Elara and Gareth stood hand in hand, looking out over the community they had helped to build. They had faced many challenges and emerged stronger for it, and now, with the support and trust of their people, they were ready to lead their alliance into a future of peace and prosperity.

The sense of accomplishment and anticipation was palpable. They were not just leaders; they were part of a greater whole, a community united by a shared vision and an unwavering commitment to each other. And with that unity, they knew they could achieve anything.

Chapter 23
Forging Ahead

The first signs of winter began to touch the village, the crisp air carrying a promise of the cold months ahead. Elara and Gareth were busy ensuring that preparations for the season were underway, overseeing the storage of food and supplies, and coordinating with the allied villages to make sure everyone was well-prepared.

Elder Brynn called for a meeting to discuss the ongoing efforts and to address any emerging concerns. The council gathered in the meeting hall, their faces reflecting a mix of determination and readiness for the challenges ahead.

"Winter is approaching, and we must ensure that all villages are adequately prepared," Elder Brynn began, his voice steady. "Our alliance has brought us strength, but we must remain vigilant and proactive."

Thomas leaned forward, his brow furrowed. "We've done well with the harvest, but we need to make sure that our supplies are distributed evenly. No village should go without."

Maren nodded in agreement. "We've set up checkpoints along the trade routes to ensure that everything runs smoothly. But we need to stay alert for any disruptions, especially with the changing weather."

Elara addressed the council, her voice calm but firm. "Our scouts have reported increased wolf activity in the northern territories. We need to bolster our defenses and ensure that our people are safe from any threats."

Anara added, "The northern villages are prepared to send additional patrols to monitor the situation. We're also coordinating with the western villages to share resources and support."

Seraphina, who had been quietly observing, spoke up. "We've seen how quickly things can change. Let's make sure we have contingency plans in place for any unexpected events."

Gareth's voice carried a note of determination. "We'll need to work closely with our allies and keep communication lines open. This winter will test our alliance, but it will also strengthen our bonds."

Elder Brynn's eyes reflected his pride in the council's unity. "We've faced many challenges together and emerged stronger each time. Let's continue to support each other and ensure that our people are well-protected and well-provided for."

As the meeting concluded, the council members dispersed to oversee the final preparations. Elara and Gareth took a moment to walk through the village, observing the hustle and bustle of activity.

Gareth's voice was thoughtful. "Winter always brings its own set of challenges. But with our alliance, we're better prepared than ever before."

Elara nodded, her eyes scanning the busy scene. "We've built something strong and resilient. As long as we continue to work together, we'll get through this winter and whatever comes next."

The preparations for winter were well underway, but there was still much to be done. Elara and Gareth coordinated with the villagers and allied leaders, ensuring that every detail was attended to. The sense of urgency was palpable, but so was the sense of unity and shared purpose.

One evening, as they were finalizing plans for resource distribution, a messenger arrived with news from the northern territories. The leader of the northern village, a man named Keldar, had requested an urgent meeting to discuss a potential threat from a rival faction that had been stirring trouble in the region.

Elara and Gareth quickly organized a delegation to travel to the northern village. As they arrived, they were greeted by Keldar and his advisors, their faces etched with concern.

"Thank you for coming so quickly," Keldar said, his voice tense. "We've received reports of increased activity from the rival faction. They've been raiding smaller outposts and disrupting our supply lines."

Elara's expression was serious. "This is a concerning development. We need to assess the situation and decide on a course of action."

Gareth added, "Our alliance is built on mutual support. We'll work together to address this threat and ensure the safety of all our people."

Keldar nodded, his relief evident. "Your support means a great deal. We've been fortifying our defenses, but we could use additional resources and fighters."

Maren, who had accompanied them, spoke up. "The western villages are prepared to send reinforcements. We'll also coordinate with the central and southern territories to ensure that our response is swift and effective."

Anara added, "We've dealt with similar threats before. With our combined strength, we can neutralize this faction and restore stability to the region."

Seraphina, ever the strategist, suggested a detailed plan. "We should gather intelligence on their movements and strategies. A coordinated strike at their key positions could disrupt their operations and force them to retreat."

Elara's voice was filled with resolve. "Let's organize scouting parties and gather as much information as possible. We'll need to move quickly to counter this threat."

Gareth nodded in agreement. "We'll send word to our allies and prepare our forces. This faction will soon learn the strength of our unity."

The leaders spent the next few hours planning and strategizing, their focus unwavering. The sense of urgency was balanced by a deep-seated confidence in their collective strength and resolve.

As the meeting concluded, Keldar expressed his gratitude. "Your support and leadership are invaluable. Together, we will overcome this challenge."

Elara and Gareth exchanged a determined look. "We've faced many challenges before, and we've always emerged stronger," Elara said. "This will be no different. Our unity is our greatest asset."

Gareth's voice was filled with conviction. "Together, we can face any threat. Let's move forward with determination and ensure the safety and prosperity of our people."

As they left the meeting hall, the sense of purpose and solidarity was stronger than ever. They were ready to face whatever challenges lay ahead, confident in their shared vision and unwavering commitment to each other and their people.

The village's preparations for winter were nearly complete when alarming news arrived. Scouts from the northern territories reported increased raids from a previously dormant faction. These attacks threatened the fragile peace and stability that the alliance had worked so hard to achieve. Elara and Gareth, accompanied by Seraphina, immediately called a council meeting to address this new threat.

The council gathered in the meeting hall, their expressions reflecting a mix of concern and determination. Elder Brynn began the discussion. "We have troubling news. Our scouts report that a rival faction has become increasingly aggressive, targeting our outposts and supply lines. We need to respond swiftly and decisively."

Thomas spoke up, his voice filled with urgency. "These raids are well-coordinated. It's clear they're trying to destabilize us before winter fully sets in. We can't let that happen."

Maren nodded, her eyes serious. "We need to fortify our defenses and ensure that our supply routes are secure. We should also consider sending reinforcements to the northern territories."

Anara added, "The northern villages are more vulnerable due to their proximity to the faction's territory. They need our support more than ever."

Elara, her voice calm but firm, addressed the council. "Our strength lies in our unity. We've faced threats before and emerged stronger. This time will be no different. Let's organize a coordinated response."

Gareth leaned forward, his expression determined. "We need a plan that combines defense with intelligence gathering. We should know exactly what we're up against before launching any counterattacks."

Seraphina, ever the strategist, outlined a plan. "We should send scouting parties to gather detailed information on their movements and strategies. At the same time, we can begin fortifying key positions and preparing our fighters."

Elder Brynn's eyes reflected his confidence in their abilities. "Agreed. We must act swiftly but wisely. Elara and Gareth, you will lead the response. Coordinate with our allies and ensure that we're prepared for any eventuality."

As the meeting concluded, Elara and Gareth moved to organize their forces. They gathered the best scouts and fighters, outlining the strategy and emphasizing the importance of unity and vigilance.

Gareth addressed the assembled scouts. "Your mission is crucial. Gather as much information as you can about the faction's movements, numbers, and strategies. We need to know what we're dealing with."

Elara added, "Be careful and stay hidden. Once we have the information, we can plan our next move. Our goal is to protect our people and ensure that our alliance remains strong."

The scouts nodded, their faces set with determination. As they set out, Elara and Gareth turned their attention to the village's defenses, ensuring that every detail was attended to.

Seraphina approached them, her expression thoughtful. "We should also consider the possibility of internal support for this faction. It's unlikely they've been able to organize so quickly without help from within."

Elara nodded. "Agreed. We need to remain vigilant and ensure that our own ranks are secure. Trust is essential, but so is caution."

Gareth's voice was resolute. "We'll monitor the situation closely. Anyone found aiding the enemy will be dealt with swiftly. Our priority is the safety and stability of our people."

With the plan in motion, the village settled into a tense but determined rhythm. The scouts returned periodically with updates, each report adding to their understanding of the threat.

As the scouts' reports came in, the council reconvened to discuss the gathered intelligence and finalize their strategy. The room buzzed with a mixture of anxiety and anticipation, each leader keenly aware of the importance of their next moves.

Thomas started the discussion, his voice grave. "The scouts have confirmed that the faction's base is well-fortified and strategically located. They're heavily armed and have been receiving supplies from an unknown source."

Maren added, "Their numbers are larger than we anticipated. A direct assault would be costly. We need a plan that minimizes our losses and maximizes our impact."

Anara's eyes were thoughtful. "We could cut off their supply lines first. Starve them out before launching a full attack. It would weaken their defenses and morale."

Seraphina agreed. "We should also create diversions to draw their forces out. A multi-pronged approach will stretch their defenses and create opportunities for us to strike."

Elara turned to Gareth, her voice steady. "We'll need to coordinate closely with our allies. Ensure that each village knows their role and is prepared to move quickly."

Gareth nodded, his expression determined. "I'll handle the coordination. We'll set up a communication network using signal fires and messengers. Speed and clarity will be crucial."

Elder Brynn's voice carried a note of urgency. "Time is of the essence. We must act before winter fully sets in. Elara and Gareth, you will lead the main force. Thomas and Maren will handle the diversions and supply line disruptions."

As the council members left to prepare their respective roles, Elara and Gareth gathered their fighters, explaining the plan and emphasizing the importance of unity and precision.

Gareth addressed the fighters, his voice filled with resolve. "This is a coordinated effort. Each of you knows your role. Trust in your training and in each other. We're fighting for our homes, our families, and our future."

Elara added, "Stay focused and stay strong. We've faced great challenges before and emerged victorious. This time will be no different. Together, we are unstoppable."

As the fighters prepared to move out, Seraphina approached Elara and Gareth, her expression serious. "I'll lead the scouting party and keep you updated on the enemy's movements. We need to stay one step ahead."

Elara nodded. "Thank you, Seraphina. Your insights and leadership have been invaluable. Stay safe and stay vigilant."

Gareth's voice was filled with confidence. "We'll coordinate our efforts and ensure that every aspect of the plan is executed flawlessly. This is our moment to show the strength of our alliance."

The village buzzed with activity as the fighters and scouts set out, each person committed to their role in the upcoming battle. The sense of unity and shared purpose was palpable, each person driven by the knowledge that they were fighting for something greater than themselves.

As night fell, Elara and Gareth stood together, watching the preparations with a sense of pride and determination. They knew the road ahead would be difficult, but they were ready to face whatever challenges came their way.

"We've prepared for this," Elara said softly, her eyes reflecting the flickering torchlight. "We're ready."

Gareth squeezed her hand, his voice steady. "Together, we'll succeed. Together, we're unstoppable."

As the first light of dawn broke over the horizon, the village moved into action, each step carefully coordinated and executed. The battle plan was in motion, and with their unity and determination, they were ready to face the threat head-on.

Chapter 24
Confrontation and Resolution

The morning was crisp, the air filled with the tension of impending conflict. Elara and Gareth stood at the forefront of their assembled fighters, each person ready for the battle ahead. The allied villages had come together, their strength and determination palpable. As the signal fires were lit, messages flew back and forth, ensuring that every group was in position.

Elara addressed the fighters, her voice strong and unwavering. "Today, we face a formidable enemy. They seek to destabilize our alliance and threaten our way of life. But we stand together, united by our commitment to each other and to our future. Remember your training, trust in each other, and fight with everything you have."

Gareth added, his voice echoing across the assembled warriors. "We've prepared for this moment. Each of you knows your role. Stay focused, stay strong, and we will prevail. For our homes, for our families, for our future."

Seraphina, standing beside them, nodded in agreement. "Our scouts have reported that the enemy is heavily fortified but disorganized. We have the element of surprise. Use it to our advantage. Strike hard, strike fast, and don't give them a chance to regroup."

Thomas stepped forward, his voice filled with determination. "We'll handle the diversions and cut off their supply lines. This will create the chaos we need for our main force to break through."

Maren, her eyes blazing with resolve, added, "The western villages are ready. We'll hit them from the flanks and keep their forces divided. They won't know what hit them."

Anara's voice was calm but firm. "Our strength lies in our unity. Let's show them what we're capable of when we stand together."

The fighters nodded, their faces set with determination. As the first rays of dawn broke through the trees, the signal was given. The allied forces moved out, each group heading to their designated positions. Elara and Gareth led the main force, their hearts pounding with a mix of anticipation and resolve.

As they approached the enemy's stronghold, they saw the smoke rising from the fires set by Thomas and his team. The sound of battle echoed through the forest, the clash of steel and the cries of warriors filling the air.

Gareth signaled to his fighters. "This is it. Remember the plan. Stay close, stay sharp."

Elara's voice cut through the din. "For our alliance, for our future!"

They charged forward, their movements precise and coordinated. The enemy, caught off guard by the simultaneous attacks, struggled to mount a coherent defense. Elara and Gareth led their fighters into the heart of the stronghold, cutting through the enemy ranks with relentless determination.

Amidst the chaos, Elara spotted the enemy leader, a tall, imposing figure directing his fighters. "There he is," she shouted to Gareth. "We need to take him down."

Gareth nodded. "Follow me. We'll cut through his guards and take him out."

With a fierce battle cry, they fought their way towards the leader, their movements a seamless dance of strength and precision. The enemy fighters, though skilled, were no match for the combined might of Elara and Gareth.

Finally, they reached the enemy leader, who turned to face them, his eyes filled with hatred. "You think you can defeat me?" he sneered. "You're fools."

Elara's voice was steady, her gaze unwavering. "We're not here for glory. We're here to protect our people and ensure a future of peace."

Gareth's voice echoed her resolve. "Your reign of terror ends today."

The battle was fierce, the enemy leader a formidable opponent. But Elara and Gareth fought with the strength and determination of their shared bond, each movement synchronized and powerful. With a final, decisive strike, they disarmed the leader, their blades at his throat.

"It's over," Elara said, her voice filled with conviction.

The enemy leader's eyes were filled with rage and fear. "This isn't the end," he spat. "Others will rise to take my place."

Gareth's gaze was cold and unyielding. "We'll be ready for them. Together, we're unstoppable."

As the enemy forces realized their leader had fallen, their resolve crumbled. The allied fighters pressed their advantage, securing the stronghold and ensuring no escape routes remained open. The battle, though intense, was over quickly. The enemy, now leaderless and demoralized, surrendered or fled into the forest.

Elara and Gareth gathered their fighters, assessing the situation and tending to the wounded. Seraphina approached, her face a mix of exhaustion and relief. "We did it. The stronghold is secure, and the enemy is in disarray."

Thomas, his face streaked with sweat and dirt, added, "Their supply lines are cut off. They won't be able to regroup anytime soon."

Maren, her voice filled with pride, said, "Our strategy worked perfectly. Each village played their part to perfection."

Anara nodded, her eyes reflecting the shared victory. "This was a true test of our alliance, and we passed with flying colors. Our unity is our greatest strength."

Elder Brynn, who had joined them after ensuring the village's safety, addressed the gathered fighters. "You've all shown incredible courage and determination. This victory belongs to all of us. Let's honor our fallen and ensure that their sacrifice was not in vain."

Elara and Gareth stood together, their hearts swelling with pride and relief. They had faced a formidable enemy and emerged victorious, their alliance stronger than ever.

Elara spoke, her voice carrying across the assembled fighters. "We've proven that together, we can overcome any challenge. This victory is a testament to our unity and our commitment to each other."

Gareth added, "Let's ensure that we remain vigilant and prepared for any future threats. Our strength lies in our unity, and we must continue to build on that foundation."

As the fighters began to tend to the wounded and secure the stronghold, Elara and Gareth took a moment to reflect on the battle. They had faced many challenges together, and each victory had brought them closer, strengthening their bond and their resolve.

Seraphina approached, her expression one of quiet satisfaction. "You both led with courage and wisdom. Our alliance is stronger because of your leadership."

Elara smiled, feeling the weight of their achievements. "We've all played a part in this victory. Our strength lies in our unity and our shared vision for the future."

Gareth nodded, his gaze steady. "We'll continue to work together, to support each other, and to build a future of peace and prosperity."

As they looked out over the battlefield, the sense of accomplishment and hope was palpable. They had faced a formidable enemy and emerged victorious, their alliance stronger than ever. Together, they were ready to face whatever challenges lay ahead, confident in their shared vision and unwavering commitment to each other and their people.

With the stronghold secured and the enemy forces scattered, Elara, Gareth, and their allies began the task of consolidating their victory. The air was filled with a mix of relief and the hum of activity as fighters tended to the wounded, fortified their positions, and prepared for any potential counterattacks.

Elder Brynn called a council meeting in the newly secured stronghold's main hall. The leaders gathered, their expressions a mix of exhaustion and determination. Elara and Gareth stood at the head of the table, ready to discuss the next steps.

Elder Brynn spoke first, his voice steady. "We have secured a significant victory today, but our work is far from over. We need to ensure that this stronghold remains in our control and that we address any lingering threats."

Thomas, his face set with determination, added, "Our scouts report that the enemy's remnants are retreating into the forest. We need to track them and ensure they can't regroup."

Maren nodded, her eyes serious. "We should also fortify this stronghold and use it as a base of operations. It's strategically important and will help us maintain control of the region."

Anara's voice was calm but firm. "We must also address the needs of our people. Many are injured, and we need to ensure they receive the care they need. We can't afford to lose anyone to preventable injuries."

Seraphina, always the strategist, suggested, "We should also send envoys to the surrounding villages to ensure they understand that the threat has been neutralized. This will prevent panic and ensure that everyone remains calm and united."

Elara turned to Gareth, her voice filled with resolve. "We need to coordinate our efforts and ensure that every aspect of our plan is executed smoothly. Let's assign tasks and get to work."

Gareth nodded, his eyes meeting those of the gathered leaders. "Thomas, take a team and track the enemy remnants. Ensure they can't regroup and pose a threat. Maren, oversee the fortification of the stronghold. Anara, organize medical teams and ensure the wounded are cared for. Seraphina, you and I will handle the communication with the surrounding villages and coordinate our defenses."

The leaders nodded in agreement, each understanding the importance of their role. As they dispersed to carry out their tasks, Elara and Gareth remained behind to discuss the broader strategy.

Elara's voice was thoughtful. "We've achieved a great victory today, but we need to remain vigilant. This stronghold is a significant asset, and we need to ensure it remains under our control."

Gareth's gaze was steady. "We'll fortify our defenses and keep our forces ready. Any attempt to retake this stronghold will be met with overwhelming force."

As they continued to discuss their plans, Seraphina approached, her expression one of quiet determination. "We've already sent word to the surrounding villages. They're relieved to hear that the threat has been neutralized, but we need to maintain a strong presence to ensure their continued confidence."

Elara nodded, her eyes reflecting her resolve. "We'll do whatever it takes to ensure the safety and stability of our people. Our strength lies in our unity, and we must continue to build on that foundation."

Gareth placed a hand on her shoulder, his voice filled with conviction. "Together, we can face any challenge. Let's get to work and ensure that this victory is just the beginning of a new era of peace and prosperity."

As the days passed, the village and its allies worked tirelessly to secure their hard-won peace. The stronghold was fortified, and the surrounding area was patrolled regularly to ensure that no remnants of the enemy could regroup. The wounded were cared for, and the villages began to return to a semblance of normalcy.

Elara and Gareth spent their days overseeing these efforts, ensuring that every detail was attended to. One afternoon, as they walked through the bustling village, they took a moment to reflect on their journey and the challenges they had overcome.

Elara's voice was filled with a mix of pride and exhaustion. "We've come so far, Gareth. From the first days of our alliance to this moment, we've faced countless challenges and emerged stronger each time."

Gareth nodded, his eyes reflecting the same sense of accomplishment. "We've built something truly remarkable. Our unity has been our greatest strength, and it's carried us through the darkest times."

As they continued their walk, they encountered Thomas, who was coordinating the fortification efforts. He greeted them with a nod. "The stronghold is nearly impregnable now. We've fortified the walls and set up patrols to ensure its security."

Elara smiled. "You've done an excellent job, Thomas. This stronghold will be a symbol of our strength and determination."

Maren approached, her face lit with excitement. "We've also started rebuilding some of the damaged villages. The people are eager to return to their homes and start anew."

Anara joined them, her voice filled with optimism. "The medical teams have done an incredible job. Most of the wounded are recovering well, and the morale of our people is high."

Seraphina, who had been overseeing the communication with the surrounding villages, added, "The news of our victory has spread, and the surrounding villages are eager to strengthen their ties with us. This alliance is becoming a beacon of hope for the entire region."

Elara's heart swelled with pride as she listened to the updates. "This is just the beginning. We've proven that we can overcome any challenge through unity and determination. Let's continue to build on this foundation and ensure that our people can live in peace and prosperity."

Gareth's voice was filled with conviction. "We've faced the storm and emerged stronger. Together, we can achieve anything. Let's keep moving forward, one step at a time."

As they walked through the village, the sense of hope and unity was palpable. The people, once divided and uncertain, now stood together, ready to face whatever the future held. Elara and Gareth knew that their journey was far from over, but with their unwavering commitment to each other and their people, they were ready for whatever challenges lay ahead.

They had built a legacy of strength, courage, and enduring hope. And with each passing day, that legacy grew stronger, fueled by the unity and determination of their people. Together, they would continue to forge a path toward a future of peace and prosperity, always ready to face the challenges and opportunities that lay ahead.

Chapter 25
A New Dawn

The days had settled into a peaceful rhythm as the alliance villages continued to strengthen their bonds and prepare for the winter ahead. The crisp air carried a sense of renewal, and the villagers worked diligently, knowing that their unity had secured a promising future. Elara and Gareth were at the center of these efforts, their leadership inspiring hope and confidence.

One morning, as Elara and Gareth were discussing the final preparations for the winter, a messenger arrived with an urgent missive. The young man, breathless from his hurried journey, handed the sealed parchment to Gareth.

Gareth broke the seal and quickly scanned the contents, his expression shifting from curiosity to concern. Elara watched him closely, sensing the gravity of the message.

"What is it?" she asked, her voice calm but firm.

Gareth looked up, meeting her eyes. "It's from the southern territories. They've discovered a significant threat—another faction that we hadn't accounted for. They request an immediate council meeting."

Elara's brow furrowed as she considered the implications. "We thought we had neutralized all immediate threats. This complicates things."

Seraphina, who had been nearby and overheard the exchange, stepped forward. "We need to assess this threat quickly. If they're reaching out, it means the situation is dire."

Gareth nodded. "I agree. We should convene the council and discuss our response. We can't afford to be caught off guard."

Within the hour, the council was assembled in the meeting hall. Elder Brynn opened the session, his voice carrying a tone of urgency. "We've received troubling news from the southern territories. A new faction has emerged, posing a significant threat to our alliance. We need to determine our course of action."

Thomas leaned forward, his face set in a determined expression. "What do we know about this faction? How are they different from the ones we've faced before?"

Gareth recounted the contents of the missive. "They are well-organized and have a strong military presence. Their tactics are more sophisticated, and they seem to be well-funded. This isn't a ragtag group of raiders; it's a well-coordinated force."

Maren's eyes narrowed. "We need to gather more intelligence. We can't rush into this without knowing what we're up against."

Anara spoke up, her voice filled with resolve. "I can send our best scouts to the southern territories. They can gather information and report back. We need to know their numbers, their resources, and their intentions."

Seraphina added, "We should also strengthen our defenses here. If this faction is as powerful as it seems, they could pose a threat to all our villages."

Elara nodded, her mind racing with the possibilities. "Agreed. We'll send scouts to gather intelligence and prepare our defenses. Let's also reach out to our allies and ensure that they're ready to support us if needed."

Elder Brynn's eyes reflected his deep concern but also his unwavering confidence in their collective strength. "We've faced many challenges before and emerged stronger. This will be no different. Let's move forward with determination and unity."

As the council dispersed to carry out their tasks, Elara and Gareth took a moment to discuss their next steps privately.

"We need to be prepared for anything," Gareth said, his voice filled with resolve. "This new faction could be a significant threat, but we've overcome great odds before."

Elara nodded, her eyes reflecting her determination. "We'll face this together, as we always have. Our strength lies in our unity and our unwavering commitment to each other and our people."

The scouts were dispatched swiftly, their mission clear and urgent. Elara and Gareth, along with Seraphina and Thomas, focused on rallying their allies and fortifying their defenses. Messages were sent to the allied villages, urging them to prepare for a potential threat and to stand ready to offer support.

Days passed, filled with intense preparations and anxious anticipation. The village buzzed with activity, each person playing their part to ensure their collective safety. The sense of unity and shared purpose was palpable, each action driven by the knowledge that their strength lay in their togetherness.

Finally, the scouts returned, bringing with them detailed reports on the new faction. Elara and Gareth convened the council once more to discuss the findings.

The lead scout, a seasoned warrior named Lyria, stood before the council, her expression grim. "The faction is indeed well-organized and heavily armed. They have a stronghold to the south, heavily fortified and strategically positioned. Their leader, a man named Kael, is a former military commander with significant resources at his disposal."

Elder Brynn's voice was steady but serious. "What are their intentions? Do we know why they've mobilized now?"

Lyria nodded. "They seem to be expanding their territory, looking to control key trade routes and resources. They've already taken over several smaller villages, forcing the inhabitants to either join them or leave."

Thomas's eyes blazed with determination. "We can't allow them to continue this. We need to strike before they gain more ground."

Maren added, "We should also reach out to those displaced by their actions. Offering them refuge and support will strengthen our alliance and undermine Kael's efforts."

Anara's voice was filled with resolve. "We'll need a coordinated strategy to take down their stronghold. It won't be easy, but with our combined forces, we can do it."

Seraphina, ever the strategist, suggested, "We should also consider cutting off their supply lines and disrupting their communications. Weakening them from within will give us a significant advantage."

Elara and Gareth exchanged a look, their determination mirrored in each other's eyes. Elara spoke, her voice filled with conviction. "We'll reach out to our allies and prepare for a coordinated strike. This threat is significant, but we've faced great challenges before and emerged stronger. Together, we will protect our people and ensure a future of peace and prosperity."

Gareth nodded, his voice steady and confident. "Let's move forward with our preparations. We have the strength, the unity, and the resolve to overcome this threat. Together, we are unstoppable."

As the council members dispersed to carry out their tasks, the sense of urgency and determination was palpable. Elara and Gareth stood at the center of it all, ready to lead their people through the coming storm, confident in their unity and their shared vision for the future.

The following days were a whirlwind of activity as Elara, Gareth, and their allies prepared for the impending conflict. The village square became a hub of coordination and planning, with leaders from the allied territories arriving to lend their support. The sense of urgency was palpable, but so was the determination to protect their lands and people.

Elara and Gareth gathered the key leaders for a final strategy meeting. The room buzzed with tension as everyone took their seats, ready to discuss the plan of action. Elder Brynn opened the meeting, his voice steady and authoritative.

"We've gathered the intelligence we need, and now it's time to finalize our strategy. Our goal is to neutralize this new faction before they can further destabilize our region."

Thomas spoke first, his voice filled with resolve. "Our scouts have identified key weaknesses in their defenses. Their supply lines are vulnerable, and their communications are disorganized. We should strike these points simultaneously to create maximum disruption."

Maren nodded in agreement. "We've also gathered resources and fighters from the western villages. We can use these forces to reinforce our main attack and ensure that we maintain the upper hand."

Anara added, "The northern villages are prepared to send additional troops and supplies. We've also set up a network of messengers to keep communication lines open during the battle."

Seraphina, always the strategist, outlined her plan. "We'll need to divide our forces into three main groups. The first group will target the supply lines, cutting off their resources. The second group will create diversions to draw their forces away from the stronghold. The third group, led by Elara and Gareth, will infiltrate the stronghold and take out their leadership."

Elara's voice was calm but firm as she addressed the group. "Our strength lies in our unity. Each of us has a crucial role to play in this battle. We've faced great challenges before, and we've always emerged stronger. This time will be no different."

Gareth added, "We need to stay focused and communicate effectively. Trust in each other and in the plan. Together, we can achieve victory."

The leaders nodded in agreement, their faces reflecting a mix of determination and readiness. As they dispersed to relay the plan to their respective forces, Elara and Gareth took a moment to speak privately with Seraphina.

Seraphina's voice was filled with quiet confidence. "We've planned for every contingency, but remember, flexibility will be key. We may need to adapt quickly as the situation evolves."

Elara nodded, her eyes reflecting her resolve. "We're ready. Our people are ready. This is our chance to protect what we've built and ensure a future of peace."

Gareth's voice was steady and reassuring. "We'll face this together, as we always have. Our unity is our greatest strength."

As the preparations continued, the village buzzed with activity. Fighters gathered their weapons, supplies were distributed, and final instructions were given. The sense of shared purpose and determination was palpable, each person committed to the success of the mission.

The dawn of the battle day was crisp and clear. The allied forces assembled at the edge of the village, ready to march towards the enemy stronghold. The atmosphere was tense but charged with a sense of unity and resolve.

Elara and Gareth moved among the fighters, offering words of encouragement and final instructions. As the signal to move out was given, the forces marched forward, their steps synchronized and purposeful.

As they approached the enemy stronghold, they split into their designated groups. Thomas led the first group towards the supply lines, his fighters moving swiftly and silently through the forest. The sound of their coordinated attack soon filled the air, the enemy caught off guard by the sudden assault.

Maren's group moved to create diversions, setting fires and launching surprise attacks that drew the enemy forces away from their positions. The chaos and confusion were evident, the enemy scrambling to respond.

Elara and Gareth led the main force towards the stronghold, their movements precise and determined. They breached the outer defenses with relative ease, their fighters cutting through the enemy ranks with practiced efficiency.

Inside the stronghold, the battle intensified. Elara and Gareth fought side by side, their movements a seamless dance of strength and precision. They encountered heavy resistance, but their determination and unity drove them forward.

Amidst the chaos, Elara spotted Kael, the enemy leader, directing his forces. She signaled to Gareth, and together they pushed through the enemy lines, their fighters providing cover.

As they closed in on Kael, he turned to face them, his eyes filled with defiance. "You think you can defeat me? Your unity means nothing."

Elara's voice was steady, her gaze unwavering. "We fight for our people and our future. Your tyranny ends today."

Gareth's voice echoed her conviction. "Your reign of terror is over. Surrender, and we may show mercy."

Kael sneered, raising his weapon. "Mercy is for the weak."

The ensuing battle was fierce and brutal. Kael fought with the desperation of a man who knew his time was up, but Elara and Gareth's combined strength and determination proved overwhelming. With a final, decisive strike, Elara disarmed Kael, her blade at his throat.

"It's over," she said, her voice filled with resolve.

Kael's eyes burned with hatred, but he knew he was beaten. "This isn't the end. Others will rise."

Gareth's gaze was cold and unyielding. "We'll be ready for them. Our unity will always prevail."

As Kael was taken into custody, the allied forces secured the stronghold. The enemy, leaderless and demoralized, surrendered or fled into the forest. The battle, though intense, was over, and the allied forces emerged victorious.

Elara and Gareth stood together, their hearts swelling with pride and relief. They had faced a formidable enemy and emerged stronger, their unity unbroken.

Elara addressed the gathered fighters, her voice carrying across the battlefield. "Today, we have shown the true strength of our alliance. This victory belongs to all of us. Let's honor our fallen and ensure that their sacrifice was not in vain."

Gareth added, "We've proven that together, we can overcome any challenge. Let's continue to build on this foundation of unity and ensure a future of peace and prosperity for all our people."

The fighters cheered, their voices ringing out in celebration. The sense of unity and shared purpose was stronger than ever, each person proud of their contribution to the victory.

As the sun set, casting a golden glow over the battlefield, Elara and Gareth looked out over their people, their hearts filled with hope and determination. They had faced a great challenge and emerged victorious, their bond and their community stronger than ever.

Together, they would continue to lead their people into a future of peace and prosperity, ready to face whatever challenges lay ahead with the same unwavering resolve and unity that had brought them this far.

Conclusion

As the dawn broke over the village, a sense of profound calm settled in. The battle against the Shadow King had ended, and with it, the oppressive darkness that had plagued their lives. The villagers began to emerge from their homes, their faces etched with a mixture of relief and wonder. The air, once heavy with fear, was now filled with the fresh scent of hope and renewal.

Elara stood at the edge of the forest, the heartstone still glowing faintly around her neck. Gareth stood beside her, his arm wrapped protectively around her shoulders. They watched as the first light of the new day spread across the village, illuminating the faces of the people they had fought so hard to protect.

"We did it," Elara whispered, her voice filled with awe. "We really did it."

Gareth smiled, his blue eyes reflecting the morning light. "We did it together, Elara. You were incredible."

Elder Brynn approached them, his face showing signs of weariness but his eyes bright with pride. "You both have done more than just defeat the Shadow King. You have united this village and shown us all that hope and courage can overcome even the darkest of times."

Elara looked at the elder, her heart swelling with gratitude. "Thank you, Brynn. We couldn't have done it without your guidance."

Brynn shook his head, a warm smile on his face. "You had the strength within you all along. I merely helped you find it."

As the villagers began to gather around, offering their thanks and praise, Elara felt a sense of belonging she had never known before. The fear and suspicion that had once surrounded her were replaced with admiration and respect. She was no longer the cursed girl on the outskirts; she was a hero, a protector of her people.

Gareth took Elara's hand, squeezing it gently. "What now, Elara? The Shadow King is gone, but there will always be challenges ahead."

Elara looked out at the horizon, the rising sun casting a golden glow over the land. "We will face them together, Gareth. With the strength of this village and the bond we share, I know we can overcome anything."

As the morning light continued to spread, the village began to come alive with the sounds of rebuilding and renewal. Children played in the streets, their laughter a melody of hope. Men and women worked together to repair the damage, their faces determined and resolute.

Elara and Gareth stood hand in hand, ready to face whatever the future held. Their journey had been long and fraught with danger, but they had emerged stronger, united by a bond that could never be broken. Together, they would continue to protect their home, their love a beacon of light against the darkness.

And so, in the peaceful dawn of a new day, the village of shadows found its way back to the light, guided by the courage and strength of two souls destined to change their world forever.

Printed by Libri Plureos GmbH in Hamburg,
Germany